Randiana

Randiana
or Excitable Tales

Profundis Publishing

Randiana, or Excitable Tales
by an anonymous author
First published 1884
Photo on cover from Pxhere
This work of fiction is in public domain
This edition copyright © 2019 Profundis Publishing
ISBN: 9-781-0709-4444-9

CHAPTER 1

A FIRST EXPERIENCE

Those of my readers who peruse the following pages and expect to find a pretty tale of surpassing interest, embellished with all the spice which fiction can suggest and a clever pen supply, will be egregiously mistaken, and had better close the volume at once. I am a plain matter-of-fact man, and relate only that which is strictly true, so that no matter how singular some of my statements may appear to those who have never passed through a similar experience, the avouchment that it is a compendium of pure fact may serve to increase the zest with which I hope it may be read.

I was born some fifty years ago in the little town of H-, about seven miles from the sea, and was educated at the grammar school, an old foundation institute, almost as old as the town itself.

Up to the age of sixteen I had remained in perfect ignorance of all those little matters which careful parents are so anxious to conceal from their children; nor, indeed, should I then have had my mind enlarged had it not been for the playful instincts of my mother's housemaid, Emma, a strapping but comely wench of nineteen, who, confined to the house all the week and only allowed out for a few hours on Sunday, could find no vent for those passionate impulses which a well-fed, full-blooded girl of her years is bound to be subject to occasionally, and more especially after the menstrual period.

It was, I remember well, at one of these times that I was called early by my mother one morning and told to go and wake Emma up, as she had overslept herself, and the impression produced upon me as barefooted and in my nightshirt I stepped into the girl's room and caught her changing the linen bandage she had been wearing round her fanny was electrical.

'Good gracious, Emma,' I said, 'what is the matter? You will bleed to death.' And in my anxiety to be of assistance, I tried to get hold of the rag where the dark crimson flood had saturated it worst.

In my haste my finger slipped in, rag and all, and my alarm was so great that had it not been for Emma laughing I believe I should have rushed downstairs and awakened the whole house.

'Don't you be a little fool, Master Jimmy,' said Emma, 'but come up tonight when your father and mother are both gone to bed, and I'll show you how it all occurred. I see you're quite ready to take a lesson,' she added, grinning, for my natural instinct had supervened on my first panic, and my nightshirt was standing out as though a good old-fashioned tent pole were underneath.

I had been frequently chafed at school about the size of my penis, which was unnaturally large for a boy of my years, but I have since found that it was an hereditary gift in our family, my father and younger brothers all boasting instruments of enormous build.

I turned reluctantly to leave the bedroom, but found it impossible to analyse my feelings, which were tumultuous and strange.

I had caught sight of a little bush of hair on the bottom of Emma's belly, and it perplexed me exceedingly.

Impelled by an impulse I could not then comprehend, but which is understandable enough now, I threw myself into Emma's arms and kissed her with fond ardour, my hands resting on two milk-white globes which peeped above the edge of her chemise. Just then I heard my mother's voice'James, what are you doing up there?'

'Nothing, mamma; I was only waking Emma up.' And I came downstairs hurriedly, with my boy's brain on fire and longing for the night, which might, I thought, make plain to me all this mystery.

That day at school appeared a dream and the time hung heavily; I went mechanically through my lessons, but seemed dazed and thoughtful; indeed so much so that I was the subject of general remark.

One of the boys, Thompson, the dull boy of the class, who was nearly seventeen, came to me after school was over and enquired what was the matter.

I suddenly resolved to ask Thompson; he was my senior and

might know.

'Can you tell me,' I said, 'the difference between a boy and a girl?'

This was too much for Thompson, who began to split with uncontrollable laughter.

'Good God, Clinton,' he said (he swore horribly), 'what a question. But I forgot you have only one sister, and she's in long clothes.'

'Well,' I replied, 'but what has that to do with it?'

'Why, everything,' said Thompson, 'if you'd been brought up among girls you'd have seen all they've got, and then you'd be as wise as other boys. Look here,' suddenly stopping and taking out a piece of slate pencil, 'you see this?' And he drew a very good imitation of a man's prick upon his slate. 'Do you know what that is?'

'Of course I do,' I said, 'haven't I got one!'

'I hope so,' replied Thompson with a smartness I hadn't up to that time thought him to possess.

'Well, now look at this.' And he drew what appeared to me at the time to be a lengthy slit. 'Do you know what that is?'

After what I had seen in the morning I could form a shrewd guess, but I feigned complete ignorance to draw Thompson out.

'Why, that's a woman's cunt, you simpleton,' observed my schoolmate, 'and if you ever have a chance of getting hold of one, grab it, my boy, and don't be long before you fill it with what God Almighty has given you,' and he ran away and left me.

I was more astonished than ever. I had lived sixteen years in the world and had learned more since six o'clock that morning than in all the preceding time.

The reader may be assured that, although I had to go to bed tolerably early, I kept awake until I heard my father and mother safely in their room.

My mother always made it a special point to come and see that I had not thrown the covers off, as I was a restless sleeper, and on this occasion I impatiently awaited the usual scrutiny.

After carefully tucking me in I watched her final departure with beating heart, and heard her say to my father as the door closed 'He was covered tonight; last evening he was a perfect sight, his prick standing up as stiff and straight as yours ever did-and such a size, too: I can't imagine where my boys get them from. You are no pigmy, dear, it is true, but I'm sure my brothers as boys were – ' And I lost the rest of the sentence as the door closed.

Now, I thought, is about the right moment, and I slid softly out of bed and across the landing to the staircase which was to lead me to heaven.

How often since then have I likened that happy staircase to the ladder which Jacob dreamed of. I've always considered that dream an allegory: Jacob's angels must have worn petticoats or some Eastern equivalent, and the Patriarch doubtless moistened the sands of Bethel thinking about it in his sleep.

CHAPTER 2

I ASCERTAIN THE MEANING OF REAL JAM

I reached her bedroom door without mishap and found her safely ensconced in bed, but with the candle still burning.

'Come here, dear,' she said, throwing back the covers, and for the first time in my life I saw a perfectly naked woman. She had purposely left off her chemise and was stretched out there, a repast for the Gods.

I do not know that, with all my experience of Paphian delicacies since, I ever have viewed any skin more closely resembling the soft peach bloom which is the acme of coetaneous beauty.

Her plump breasts stood out as though chiselled by some cunning sculptor, but my eyes were not enchained by them. They wandered lower to that spot which to me was such a curious problem, and I said 'May I look?'

She laughed, and opening her legs, answered me without saying a word.

I examined it closely, and was more and more puzzled.

Her menses had passed and she had carefully washed away the stains.

'Put your finger in,' she said, 'it won't bite you; but haven't you really, Master Jimmy, ever seen one of these things before?'

I assured her that I had not.

'Then in that case,' said Emma, 'I shall have some virgin spoil tonight.' And passing her hand under my nightshirt, she took hold of my prick with a quick movement that surprised me, and although it was proudly erect and seemed ready to burst, she worked it up and down between her thumb and forefinger till I was fairly maddened.

'Oh! for God's sake,' I murmured, 'don't do that, I shall die.'

'Not yet, my darling,' she said, taking hold of me and lifting me, for she was a girl of enormous muscular power, on top of her. 'Not until I have eased my own pain and yours too.'

Emma called passion pain, and I have since proved her to

be some sort of a philosopher. I have carefully analysed that terrible feeling which immediately precedes the act of emission, and find pain the only proper word to express it.

I struggled with her at first, for in my innocence I scarcely knew what to make of her rapid action, but I had not long to remain in doubt.

Holding my prick in her left hand and gently easing back the prepuce, which had long since broken its ligature, though through no self-indulgence on my part, she brought it within the lips of her orifice, and then with a quick jerk which I have since thought was almost professional, I found myself buried to the extreme hilt in a sea of bliss.

I instinctively found myself moving up and down with the regular see-saw motion that friction will unconsciously compel, but I need not have moved, for Emma could have managed the whole business herself.

The movement of her hips and her hands, which firmly grasped the cheeks of my fat young arse, soon produced the desired result, and in my ecstasy I nearly fainted.

At first I thought that blood in a large quantity had passed from me and I whispered to Emma that the sheets would be stained red, and then Mamma would know, but she soon quieted my fears.

'What an extraordinary prick you have, Master James, for one so young. Why it's bigger than your father's.'

'How do you know that?' I asked, surprised more than ever.

'Well, my dear, that would be telling,' she said, 'but now that you have tried what a woman is like, what do you think of it?'

'I think it's simply splendid,' was my response; and indeed, although long years of varied experience may have dulled the wild ardour of youth, and a fuck is hardly the mad excitement which it was, I should find it difficult to improve upon the answer I gave to Emma.

Twice more I essayed valiantly to escalade the fortress of my inamorata, and each time she expressed astonishment to think a mere child should have such 'grit' in him.

All at once I heard a slight noise on the stairs, and thinking it was my mother, hastily slunk under the bed; the candle was still burning.

'Are you asleep, Emma?' whispered a low voice. It was my father's.

'Lor', sir,' she said, 'I hope the missus didn't hear you coming up. I thought you said it was to be tomorrow.'

'I did,' replied my father, 'but to tell you the truth I couldn't wait. I put a drop of laudanum in your mistress's glass of grog just before retiring, so she's safe enough.'

And this man called himself my father? I need scarcely say I lost all my respect for him from that moment.

Not another word was passed, but peeping from my hiding-place I saw by the shadow on the wall that my father was preparing for immediate action, yet he went about it a very different way from me.

He insisted upon her taking his penis into her mouth, which at first she refused, but after some little solicitation and a promise that she should go to the 'fairing' which was to be held on the following Friday, she finally consented, and to see my father's shadow wriggling about on the wall while his arse described all manner of strange and to me

unnatural contortions, was a sight that even at this distance of time never fails to raise a smile whenever I think of it.

Presently the old man shouted out, 'Hold on, Emma, that's enough, let's put it in now.'

But Emma was shrewd; she knew what a frightfully drowned-out condition her fanny was in and felt sure my father, with his experience, would smell a rat, so she held on to his tool with her teeth and refused to let go till my father, between passion and pain, forced it away from her. But judge of his disgust when he found himself spending before he could reach the seat of bliss.

His curses took my breath away.

'You silly bitch,' he said, 'you might have known I couldn't stand that long,' and still muttering despondent oaths, he got out of bed to make water.

Now unfortunately the chamber pot was close to my head, and Emma's exhaustion after the quadruple performance was so great that for the moment she forgot me.

The exclamation of my father as he stooped down and

caught sight of his eldest boy recalled her to herself.

I would rather draw a veil over the scene that ensued. Suffice it to say that Emma received a month's wages in the morning, and I was packed off to a boarding school.

My mother had not slept so soundly as my father had fondly hoped. Whether the laudanum was not of first-rate quality, or her instincts were prematurely sharp, I have never been able to determine, but I do know that before my rather had dragged me from underneath Emma's bed on that eventful night he was saluted from behind with a blow

from a little bedroom poker, which would have sent many a weaker constitutioned man to an untimely grave.

CHAPTER 3

MORAL AND DIDACTIC THOUGHTS

Having in the last two chapters related my first boyhood experience in love, I think it will equal any to be found in works of greater fame, but I do not intend to weary you with any further relations of my early successes on the Venusian warpath.

I pass over the period of my youth and very early manhood, leaving you to imagine that my first lesson with Emma and my father as joint instructors was by no means thrown away.

Yet I found at the age of thirty that I was only on the threshold of mysteries far more entrancing. I had up to that time been a mere man of pleasure, whose ample fortune (for my father, who had grown rich, did not disinherit me when he died) sufficed to procure any of those amorous delights without which the world would be a blank to me.

But further than the ordinary pleasures of the bed I had not penetrated.

'The moment was, however, approaching when all these would sink into insignificance before those greater sensual joys which wholesome and well-applied flagellation will always confer upon its devotees.' I quote the last sentence from a well-known author, but I'm far from agreeing with it in theory or principle.

I was emerging one summer's evening from the Cafe Royal in Regent Street, when De Vaux, a friend of long standing whom I was with, nodded to a gentleman passing in a hansom who at once stopped the cab and got out.

'Who is it?' I said, for I felt a sudden and inexplicable interest in his large lustrous eyes, eyes such as I have never before seen in any human being.

'That is Father Peter, of St Martha of the Angels. He is a bircher, my boy, and one of the best in London.'

At this moment we were joined by the Father and a formal introduction took place.

I had frequently seen admirable cartes of Father Peter, or

rather, as he preferred to be called, Monsignor Peter, in the shop windows of the leading photographers, and at once accused myself of being a dolt not to have recognised him at first sight.

Descriptions are wearisome at the best, yet were I a clever novelist given to the art, I think I might even interest those of the sterner sex in Monsignor Peter, but although in the following paragraph I faithfully delineate him, I humbly ask his pardon if he should perchance in the years to come glance over these pages and think I have not painted his portrait in colours sufficiently glowing, for I must assure my readers that Father Peter is no imaginary Apollo, but one who in the present year of grace, 1883, lives, moves, eats, drinks, fucks and flagellates with all the verve and dash he possessed at the date I met him first, now twenty-five years ago.

Slightly above the middle height and about my own age, or possibly a year my senior, with finely chiselled features and exquisite profile, Father Peter was what the world would term an exceedingly handsome man. It is true that perfectionists have pronounced the mouth a trifle too sensual and the cheeks a thought too plump for a standard of perfection, but the women would have deemed otherwise for the grand dreamy Oriental eyes, which would have outrivaled those of Byron's Gazelle, made up for any shortcoming.

The tonsure had been sparing in its dealings with his hair, which hung in thick but well-trimmed masses round a classic head, and as the slight summer breeze blew aside one lap of his long clerical coat, I noticed the elegant shape of his cods which, in spite of the tailor's art, displayed their proportions to the evident admiration of one or two ladies who, pretending to look in at the windows of a draper near which we were standing, seemed riveted to the spot, as the zephyrs revealed the tantalising picture.

'I am pleased to make your acquaintance, Mr. Clinton,' said Father Peter, shaking me cordially by the hand. 'Any friend of Mr. De Vaux is a friend of mine. May I ask if either of you have dined yet?'

We replied in the negative.

'Then in that case, unless you have something better to do, I shall be glad if you will join me at my own home. I dine at seven, and am already rather late. I feel half-famished and was proceeding to Kensington, where my humble quarters are, when the sight of De Vaux compelled me to discharge the cab. What say you?'

'With all my heart,' replied De Vaux, and since I knew him to be a perfect sybarite at the table, and that his answer was based on a knowledge of Monsignor's resources, I readily followed suit.

To hail a four-wheeler and get to the doors of Father Peter's handsome but somewhat secluded dwelling, which was not very far from the south end of the long walk in Kensington Gardens, did not occupy more than twenty minutes.

En route I discovered that Father Peter possessed a further charm which, added to those I have already mentioned, must have made him (as I thought even then and I know now) perfectly invincible among womankind. He was the most fascinating conversationalist I had ever listened to. It was not so much the easy winning way in which he framed his sentences, but the rich musical intonation, and the luscious laughing method he had of suggesting an infinity of things without, as a respectable member of an eminently respectable church, committing himself in words.

No one, save at exceptional intervals, could ever repeat any actual phrase of Monsignor's which might not pass in a drawing-room, yet there was an instinctive craving on the part of his audience to hear more because they imagined he meant something which was going to lead up to something further, yet the something further never came.

Father Peter was wont to say when questioned upon this annoying peculiarity'Am I to be held answerable for other people's imaginations?'

But then Father Peter was a sophist of the first water, and a clever reasoner could have proved that his innuendos had created the imaginings in the first place.

Daudet, Belot, and other leaders of the French fictional school, have at times carefully analysed those fine nuances which distinguish profligate talk from delicate suggestiveness. Monsignor had read these works, and adapted their ideas with success.

'Mychef? said Monsignor as we entered the courtyard of his

residence, 'tyrannises over me worse than any Nero. I am only five minutes behind and yet I dare not ask him for an instant's grace. You are both dressed. I suppose if I hadn't met you it would have been the Royalty front row; Fiorina, they say, has taken to forgetting her unmentionables lately.'

We both denied the soft impeachment and assured him that information about Fiorina was news to us.

Monsignor professed to be surprised at this, and rushed off to his dressing-room to make himself presentable.

CHAPTER 4

A SNUG DINNER PARTY

Before many minutes he rejoined us, and leading the way, we followed him into one of the most lovely bijou salons it had ever been my lot to enter. There were seats for eight at the table, four of which were occupied, and the chef, not waiting for his lord and master, had already sent up the soup, which was being handed round by a plump rose-cheeked boy about sixteen years old, who I afterwards found acted in the double capacity of page to Monsignor and chorister at St Martha of the Angels, to say nothing of a tertiary occupation which, not to put too fine a point upon it, might go excessively near to buggery without being very wide of the mark.

I was briefly introduced, and De Vaux, who knew them all, had shaken himself into his seat before I found time properly to note the appearance of my neighbours.

Immediately on my left sat a complete counterpart of Monsignor himself, save that he was a much older man; his name, as casually mentioned to me, was Father Boniface, and although sparer in his proportions than Father Peter, his proclivities as a trencherman belied his meagreness. He never missed a single course, and when anything particular tickled his gustatory sense, he had two or even more helpings.

Next to him sat a little short apoplectic man, a doctor of medicine, who was more of an epicure.

A sylphlike girl of sixteen occupied the next seat. Her fair hair, rather flaxen than golden-hued, hung in profusion down her back, while black lashes gave her violet eyes that shade which Greuze, the finest eye painter the world has ever seen, wept to think he could never exactly reproduce. I was charmed with her ladylike manner, her neatness of dress, virgin white, and above all, with the modest and unpretending way she replied to the questions put to her.

If ever there was a maid at sixteen under the blue vault of heaven, she sits there, was my involuntary thought, to which I nearly gave verbal expression, but was fortunately saved from such a frightful lapse by the page who, placing some appetising salmon and lobster sauce before me, dispelled for the nonce my half-visionary condition.

Monsignor P. sat near this young divinity, and ever and anon between the courses passed his soft white hands through her wavy hair.

I must admit I didn't half like it, and began to feel a jealous pang, but the knowledge that it was only the caressing hand of a Father of the Romish Church quieted me.

I was rapidly getting maudlin, and as I ate my salmon the smell of the lobster sauce suggested other thoughts till I found the tablecloth gradually rising, and I was obliged to drop my napkin on the floor to give myself the opportunity of adjusting my prick so that it would not be observed by the company.

I have omitted to mention the charmer who was placed between De Vaux and Father Peter. She was a lady of far maturer years than the sylph, and might be, as near as one could judge in the pale incandescent light which the pure filtered gas shed round with voluptuous radiance, about twenty-seven. She was a strange contrast to Lucy, for so my sylph was called. Tall, and with a singularly clear complexion for a brunette, her bust was beautifully rounded with that fullness of contour which, just avoiding the gross, charms without disgusting. Madeline, in short, was in every inch a woman to chain a lover to her side.

I had patrolled the Continent in search of goods; I had overhauled every shape and make of cunt between Constantinople and Calcutta; but as I caught the liquid expression of Madeline's large sensuous eyes, I confessed myself a fool.

Here in Kensington, right under a London clubman's nose was the beau ideal had vainly travelled ten thousand miles to find. She was sprightliness itself in conversation, and I could not sufficiently thank De Vaux for having introduced me into such an Eden.

Lamb cutlets and cucumbers once more broke in upon my dream, and I was not at all sorry, for I found the violence of my thought had burst one of the buttons of my fly, a mishap I knew from past experience would be followed by the collapse of the others unless I turned my erratic brain wanderings into another channel; so I kept my eyes fixed on my plate, absolutely afraid to gaze upon these two constellations again.

'As I observed just now,' said the somewhat fussy little doctor, 'cucumber or cowcumber, it matters not much which, if philologists differ in the pronunciation surely we may.'

'The pronunciation,' said Father Peter, with a naive look at Madeline, 'is very immaterial, provided one does not eat too much of them. They are a dangerous plant, sir, they heat the blood, and we poor churchmen, who have to chastise the lusts of the flesh, should avoid them in toto; yet I would fain have some more.' And suiting the action to the word, he helped himself to a large quantity.

I should mention that I was sitting nearly opposite Lucy, and seeing her titter at the paradoxical method the worthy Father had of assisting himself to cucumber against his own argument, I thought it a favourable opportunity to show her that I sympathised with her mirth, so, stretching out my foot, I gently pressed her toe, and to my unspeakable joy she did not take her foot away, but rather, indeed, pushed it further in my direction.

I then, on the pretence of adjusting my chair, brought it a little nearer the table, and was in ecstasies when I perceived that Lucy not only guessed what my manoeuvres meant, but actually in a very sly-puss-like way brought her chair nearer too.

Then balancing my arse on the edge of my seat as far as I could without being noticed, with my prick only covered with the table napkin, for it had with one wild bound burst all the remaining buttons on my breeches, I reached forward my foot, from which I had slid off my boot with the other toe, and in less than a minute I had worked it up so that I could just feel the heat of her fanny.

I will say this for her, she tried all she could to help me, but her cursed drawers were an insuperable obstacle, and I was foiled. I knew if I proceeded another inch I should inevitably come a cropper, and this knowledge, coupled with the fact that Lucy was turning wild with excitement, now red, now white, warned me to desist for the time being.

I now foresaw a rich conquest-something worth waiting

for-and my blood coursed through my veins at the thought of the sweet little bower nestling within those throbbing thighs, for I could tell from the way her whole frame trembled how thoroughly mad she was at the trammels which society imposed. Not only that, the moisture on my stocking told me that it was something more than the dampness of perspiration, and I felt half sorry to think that I had 'jewgaged' her. At the same time, to parody the words of the poet laureate'Tis better to have frigged with one's toe, Than never to have frigged at all.

Some braised ham and roast fowls now came on, and I was astonished to find a poor priest of the Church of Rome launching out in this fashion. The sauterne with the salmon had been simply excellent, and the Mumms, clear and sparkling, which accompanied the latter courses had fairly electrified me.

By the way, as this little dinner party may serve as a lesson to some of those whose experience is limited, I will mention one strange circumstance which may account for much of what is to come.

Monsignor, when the champagne had been poured out for the first time, before anyone had tasted it, went to a little liqueur stand, and taking from it a bottle of a most peculiar shape, added to each glass a few drops of the cordial.

'That is Pinero Balsam,' he said to me, 'you and one of the ladies have not dined at my table before, and, therefore, you may possibly never have tasted it, as it is but little known in England. It is compounded by one Italian firm only, whose ancestors, the Sagas of Venice, were the holders of the original recipe. Its properties are wondrous and manifold, but amongst others it rejuvenates senility, and those among us who have travelled up and down in the world a good deal and found the motion rather tiring as the years go on, have cause to bless its recuperative qualities.'

The cunning cleric by the inflection of his voice had sufficiently indicated his meaning and although the cordial was, so far as interfering with the champagne went, apparently tasteless, its effect upon the company soon began to be noticeable.

A course of ducklings, removed by Nesselrode pudding and Noyau jelly, ended the repast, and after one of the shortest graces in Latin I had ever heard in my life, the ladies curtsied themselves out of the apartment, and soon the strains of a piano indicated that they had reached the drawing-room, while we rose from the table to give the domestics an opportunity for clearing away.

My trousers were my chief thought at this moment, but I skilfully concealed the evidence of my passion with a careless pocket handkerchief, and my boot I accounted for by a casual reference to a corn of long standing.

CHAPTER 5

THE HISTORY OF FLAGELLATION CONDENSED

'Gentlemen,' said Monsignor, lighting an exquisitely aromatised cigarette-for all priests, through the constant use of the censer, like the perfume of spices-'first of all permit me to hope that you have enjoyed your dinner; and now I presume, De Vaux, your friend will not be shocked if we initiate him into the mysteries with which we solace the few hours of relaxation our priestly employment permits us to enjoy. Eh, Boniface?'

The latter, who was coarser than his superior, laughed boisterously.

'I expect, Monsignor, that Mr. Clinton knows just as much about birching as we do ourselves.'

'I know absolutely nothing of it,' I said, 'and must even plead ignorance of the merest rudiments.'

'Well, sir,' said Monsignor, leaning back in his chair, 'die art of birching is one on which I pride myself that I can speak with greater authority than any man in Europe, and you may judge that I do not aver this from any self-conceit when I tell you that I have, during the last ten years, assisted by a handsome subsidy from the Holy Consistory at Rome, ransacked the known world for evidence in support of its history. In that escritoire,' he said, 'there are sixteen octavo volumes, the compilation of laborious research, in which I have been assisted by brethren of all the holy orders affiliated to Mother Church, and I may mention in passing that worthy Dr Price here and Father Boniface have both contributed largely from their wide store of experience in correcting and annotating many of the chapters which deal with recent discoveries; for, Mr. Clinton, flagellation as an art is not only daily gaining fresh pupils and adherents, but scarcely a month passes without some new feature being added to our already huge stock of information.'

I lighted a cigar and said I should like to hear something more about it.

'To begin with,' began Father Peter, 'we have indubitable

proof from the Canaanitish Stones found in the Plain of Shinar, in 1748, and unearthed by Professor Bannister, that the priests of Baal, more than three thousand years ago, not only practised flagellation in a crude form with hempen cords, but inculcated the practice in those who came to worship at the shrine of their god, and these are the unclean mysteries which are spoken of by Moses and Joshua, but which the Hebrew tongue had no word for.'

'You astonish me,' I said, 'but what proof have you of this?'

'Simply this: it was the age of hieroglyphics, and on the Shinar Stone was found, exquisitely carved, a figure of the god Baal gloating over a young girl whose virgin nakedness was being assailed by several stout priests with rough cords. I have a facsimile in volume 7, page 343-hand it to Mr. Clinton, Boniface.'

Boniface did so, and sure enough there was the Canaanitish presentment of a young maiden with her lovely rounded arse turned up to the sky, and her hands tied to the enormous prick of the god Baal, being soundly flogged by two stout-looking men in loose but evidently priestly vestments.

'The fact that the Israelites and men of Judah were constantly leaving their own worship, enticed away by the allurements of the Baalite priests, is another proof of the superior fascination which flagellation even in those days had over such unholy rites as sodomy.'

'Your deductions interest me as a matter of history,' I said, 'but nothing more.'

'Oh, I think I could interest you in another way presently,' said Dr Price.

Monsignor continued: 'The races all, more or less, have indulged in a love of the art, and it is well known that so far as Aryan lore will permit us to dive into the subject, both in Babylon and Nineveh, and even in later times in India also (which is surely something more than a mere coincidence), flagellation has not only thrived, but has been the fashionable recreation of all recorded time.'

'I really cannot see,' I interrupted, 'where you get your authorities from.'

'Well, so far as Nineveh goes, I simply ask you to take a

walk through the Assyrian Hall of the British Museum, where in several places you will see the monarchs of that vast kingdom sitting on their thrones and watching intently some performance which seems to interest them greatly. In the foreground you will perceive a man with a whip of knotted thongs, as much like our cat-o'-nine-tails as anything, on the point of belabouring something-and then the stone ends; in other words, where the naked-arsed Assyrian damsel would be there is nil. Of course she has been chipped off by the authorities, seeing the scene as being likely to demoralise young children, who would begin to practise on their own posteriors, and end by fucking themselves into an early grave.'

'Well,' I said, in unbounded surprise, 'your research is certainly too much for me.'

'I thought we should teach you something presently,' laughed Dr Price.

'I have thousands of examples in those sixteen volumes, from the Aborigines of Australia and the Maoris of New Zealand to the Eskimos in their icy homes, the latter of whom may be said to have acquired the art by instinct, the cold temperature of the frozen zone suggesting flagellation as a means of warmth, and indeed, in a lecture read to the Geographical Society, Mr. Wimwam proved that the frigidity of Greenland prevented the women from procreating unless flagellation, and vigorous flagellation, too, had been previously applied.

'The patristic Latin in which the books of the Holy Fathers are written,' went on Monsignor, 'contain numerous hints and examples, but although Clement of Alexandria quotes some startling theories, and both Lactantius and Tertullian back him to some extent, I cannot help thinking that so far as practical bum-tickling is concerned, we are a long way ahead of all the ancients.'

'But,' observed Dr Price mildly, 'Ambrose and Jerome knew a thing or two.'

'They had studied,' replied the imperturbable Father Peter, 'but were not cultured as we moderns are; for example, their birches grew in the hills of Illyria and Styria, and in that part of Austria we now call the Tyrol. Canada, with its glorious forests of birch, was unknown. Why, sir,' said Monsignor, turning to me, his eyes lit up with the lambent flame of enthusiasm, 'do you know the king birch of Manitoba will execute more enchantment on a girl's backside in five minutes than these old contrivances of our forefathers could have managed in half an hour? My ringers tingle when I think of it. Show him a specimen of our latest consignment, Boniface.' And the latter worthy rushed off to do his master's bidding.

To tell the truth I scarcely appreciated all this, and felt a good deal more inclined to get upstairs to the drawing-room; just at this moment an incident occurred which gave me my opportunity. The bonny brunette, Madeline, looked in at the door furtively and apologised, but reminded Monsignor that he was already late for vespers.

'My dear girl,' said the cleric, 'run over to the sacristy, and ask Brother Michael to officiate in my absence-the usual headache-and don't stay quite so long as you generally do, and if you should come back with your hair dishevelled and your dress in disorder, make up a better tale than you did last time.'

Or else your own may smart, I thought, for at this moment Father Boniface came in to ask Monsignor for another key to get the rods, as it appeared he had given him the wrong one.

Now is my time, I reflected, so making somewhat ostentatious enquiries as to the exact whereabouts of the lavatory, I quitted the apartment, promising to return in a few minutes.

I should not omit to mention that from the moment I drank the sparkling cordial that Father Peter had mixed with the champagne, my spirits had received an unwonted exhilaration, which I could not ascribe to natural causes.

I will not go so far as to assert that the augmentation offered which I found my prick to possess was entirely due to the Pinero Balsam, but this I will confidently maintain against all comers, that never had I felt so equal to any amorous exploit. It may have been the effect of a generous repast, it might have been the result of the toe-frigging I had indulged in; but as I stepped into the brilliantly lighted hall, and hastily passed upstairs to the luxurious drawing-room, I could not help congratulating myself on the stubborn bar of iron which my unfortunately dismantled trousers could scarcely keep from popping out.

CHAPTER 6

VENI, VIDI, VICI!

Fearing to frighten Lucy if I entered suddenly in a state of dishabille, and feeling certain that a prick exhibition might tend to shock her inexperienced eye, I readjusted my bollocks and peeped through the crack of the drawing-room door, which had been left temptingly half open.

There was Lucy reclining on the sofa in that dolce far niente condition which is a sure sign that a good dinner has agreed with one, and that digestion is waiting upon appetite like an agreeable and good-tempered handmaid should.

She looked so arch, and with such a charming pout upon her lips, that I stood there watching, half disinclined to disturb her dream.

It may be, I thought, that she is given to frigging herself, and being all alone she might possibly-but I speedily banished that thought, for Lucy's clear complexion and vigorous blue eyes forbade the suggestion.

At this instant something occurred which for the moment again led me to think that my frigging conjecture was about to be realised, for she reached her hand deliberately under her skirt and, lifting up her petticoats, dragged down the full length of her chemise, which she closely examined. I divined it all at a glance: when I toe-frigged her in the dining-room she had spent a trifle, and it being her first experience of the kind, she could not understand it.

So she really is a maid after all, I thought, and as I saw a pair of shapely ladylike calves encased in lovely pearl silk stockings of a light blue colour, I could restrain myself no longer, and with a couple of bounds was at her side before she could recover herself.

'Oh! Mr. Clinton. Oh! Mr. Clinton; how could you,' was all she found breath or thought to ejaculate.

I simply threw my arms around her and kissed her flushed face, on the cheeks, for I feared to frighten her too much at first.

At last, finding she lay prone and yielding, I imprinted a kiss upon her mouth, and found it returned with ardour.

Allowing my tongue gently to insinuate itself into her half-open mouth and touch hers, I immediately discovered that her excitement, as I fully expected, became doubled, and without saying a word I guided her disengaged hand to my prick, which she clutched with the tenacity of a drowning man catching at a floating spar.

'My own darling,' I said, and waiting for no further encouragement, I pushed my right hand softly up between her thighs, which mechanically opened to give it passage.

To say that I was in the seventh heaven of delight, as my warm fingers found a firm plump cunt with a rosebud hymen as yet unbroken, is but faintly to picture my ecstasy.

To pull her a little way further down on the couch so that her rounded arse would rise in the middle and make the business a more convenient one, was the work of a second; the next I had withdrawn my prick from her grasp and placed it against the lips of her quim, at the same time easing them back with a quick movement of my thumb and forefinger. I gave one desperate lunge, which made Lucy cry out 'Oh God,' and the joyful deed was consummated.

As I have hinted before, my prick was no joke in the matter of size, and upon this occasion, so intense was the excitement that had led up to the fray, it was rather bigger than usual; but thanks to the heat the sweet virgin was in, the sperm particles of her vagina were already resolved into grease, which, mixing with the few drops of blood caused by the violent separation of the hymeneal cord, resulted in making the friction natural and painless. Not only that, once inside I found Lucy's fanny was internally framed on a very free-and-easy scale-and here permit me to digress and point out the ways of nature.

Some women are framed with an orifice like an exaggerated horse collar, but with a passage more fitted for a tin whistle than a man's prick, while in others the opening itself is like the tiniest wedding ring, though if you once get inside your prick is in the same condition as the poor devil who floundered up the biggest cunt on record and found another bugger looking for his hat.

Others again-but why should I go on in this prosy fashion, when Lucy has only received half a dozen strokes, and is on the point of coming.

What a delicious process we went through; even to recall it after all these years, now that Lucy is a staid matron, the wife of a church rector, and the mother of two youths verging on manhood, is bliss, and will in my most depressed moments always suffice to give me a certain and prolonged erection.

The beseeching blue eyes that glanced up at Monsignor's drawing-room ceiling, as though in silent adoration and heartfelt praise at the warm stream I seemed to be spurting into her very vitals; the quick nervous shifting of her fleshy buttocks, as she strove to ease herself of her own pent-up store of liquid; and then the heartfelt sigh of joy and relief that escaped her ruby lips as I withdrew my tongue and she discharged the sang de la vie at the same moment.

Oh! there is no language copious enough to do justice to the acme of a first fuck, nor is there under God's sun a nation which has yet invented a term sufficiently comprehensive to picture the emotions of a man's mind as he mounts a girl he knows from digital proof to be a maid as pure in person and as innocent of prick, dildo or candle as arctic snow.

Scarcely had I dismounted and reassured Lucy with a serious kiss that it was all right, and that she need not alarm herself, when Madeline came running in.

'Oh! Lucy,' she cried, 'such fun-' Then, seeing me, she abruptly broke off with-'I beg your pardon, Mr. Clinton, I did not see you were here.'

Lucy, who was now in a sitting posture, joined in the conversation, and I saw by the ease of her manner that she had entirely recovered her self-possession, and that I could rejoin the gentlemen downstairs.

'Do tell those stupid men not to stay there over their cigars all day. It is paying us no compliment,' was Madeline's parting shot.

In another moment I was in my seat again, and prepared for a resumption of Monsignor's lecture on birch rods.

'Where the devil have you been to, Clinton?' said De Vaux.

'Where it would have been quite impossible for you to have acted as my substitute,' I unhesitatingly replied.

My answer made them all laugh, for they thought I referred to the water closet, whereas I was of course alluding to Lucy, and I knew I was stating a truism in that case as regarded De Vaux, for he was scarcely yet convalescent from a bad attack of Spanish glanders, which was always his happy method of expressing the clap.

CHAPTER 7

A VICTIM FOR THE EXPERIMENT

'Now my dear Mr. Clinton, I wish you particularly to observe the tough fibre of these rods,' said Monsignor Peter, as he handed me a bundle so perfectly and symmetrically arranged that I could not help remarking on it.

'Ah!' exclaimed Monsignor, 'that is a further proof of how popular the flagellating art has become. So large a trade is being done, sir, in specially picked birch of the flagellating kind, that they are hand-sorted by children and put up in bundles by machinery, as they appear here, and my own impression is that if the Canadian Government were to impose an extra duty on these articles, for they almost come under the heading of manufactures and not produce, a large revenue would accrue; but enough of this,' said the reverend gentleman, seeing his audience was becoming somewhat impatient. 'You saw at the dinner table the young lady I addressed as Lucy?'

I reflected for a moment to throw them off their guard, and then said, suddenly, 'Oh, yes, the sweet thing in white.'

'Well,' continued Monsignor Peter, 'her father is long dead, and her mother is in very straitened circumstances; the young girl herself is a virgin, and I have this morning paid to her mother a hundred pounds to allow her to remain in my house for a month or so with the object of initiating her.'

'Initiating her into the Church?' I enquired, laughing to myself, for I knew that her initiation in other respects was fairly well accomplished.

'No,' smiled Monsignor, touching the rods significantly, 'this is the initiation to which I refer.'

'What,' I cried, aghast, 'are you going to birch her?'

'We are,' put in Dr Price. 'Her first flagellation will be tonight, but this is merely an experimental one. A few strokes well administered, and a quick fuck after to determine my work on corpuscular action of the blood particles; tomorrow she will be in better form to receive second-stage instruction, and we hope by the end of the month-'

'To have a perfect pupil,' put in Father, who did not relish Dr Price taking the lead on a flagellation subject, 'but let us proceed to the drawing-room. Boniface, put that bundle in the birch box and bring it upstairs.'

So saying, the chief exponent of flagellation in the known world led the way upstairs to the drawing-room, and we followed, though I must confess that in my case it was with no slight trepidation, for I felt somehow as though I were about to assist at a sacrifice.

As we entered the room we found Lucy in tears, and Madeline consoling her, but she no sooner saw us than, breaking from her friend, she threw herself at Monsignor's feet, and clinging to his knees, sobbed out'Oh, Father Peter, you have always been a land friend to my mother and myself, do say that the odious tale of shame that girl has poured into my ears is not true.'

'Good God!' I muttered, 'they have actually chosen Madeline as the instrument to explain what they are about to do.'

'Rise, my child,' said Monsignor, 'do not distress yourself but listen to me.' Half bearing the form of the really terrified young thing to the couch, we gathered round in a circle and listened.

"You doubtless know, my sweet daughter,' began the wily and accomplished priest, 'that the votaries of science spare neither friends nor selves in their efforts to unravel the secrets of nature. Time and pain are no object to them, so that the end be accomplished.'

To this ominous introduction Lucy made no response.

'You have read much, daughter of mine,' said Monsignor, stroking her silken hair, 'and when I tell you that your dead father devoted you to the fold of Mother Church, and that your mother and I both think you will best be serving Her ends and purposes by submitting yourself to those tests which will be skilfully carried out without pain, but on the contrary, with an amount of pleasure such as you cannot even guess at, you will probably acquiesce.'

Lucy's eyes here caught mine, and although I strove to

reassure her with a look that plainly intimated no harm should come to her, she was some time before she at last put her hand in the cleric's and said 'Holy Father, I do not think you would allow anything very dreadful; I will submit, for my mother, when I left her this morning, told me above all else to be obedient to you in everything and to trust you implicitly.'

'That is my own trump of a girl,' said Monsignor, surprised for the first time during the entire evening into a slang expression, but I saw his large round orbs gloating over his victim, and his whole frame trembled with excitement as he led Lucy into the adjoining apartment and left her alone with Madeline.

'Now, gentlemen,' said Monsignor, 'the moment approaches, and you will forgive me, Mr. Clinton, if I have to indulge in a slight coarseness of language, but time presses, and plain Saxon is the quickest method of expression. Personally, I do not feel inclined to fuck Lucy myself, as the fact is I had connection with her mother the night previous to her marriage, and as Lucy was born exactly nine months afterwards, I am rather in doubt as to the paternity.'

'In other words,' I said, astounded, 'you think it possible that you may be her father.'

'Precisely,' said Monsignor. 'You see that the instant the flagellation is ended, somebody must necessarily fuck her, and personally my objection prevents me. Boniface, here, prefers boys to women, and Dr Price will be too busy taking notes, so that it rests between you and De Vaux, who had better toss up.'

De Vaux, who was stark mad to think that his little gonorrhoeal disturbance was an insuperable obstacle, pleaded an engagement later on, which he was bound to fulfil, and therefore Monsignor Peter told me to be sure to be ready the instant I was wanted.

Madeline entered at this moment and informed us that all was ready, but gave us to understand that she had experienced the greatest difficulty in overcoming poor Lucy's natural scruples at being exposed in all her virgin nakedness to the gaze of so many of the male sex.

'She made a very strange observation, too,' continued Madeline, looking at me with a drollery I could not understand.

'She said, "If it had been only Mr. Clinton, I don't think I should have minded quite so much."'

'Oh! all the better,' said Father Peter, 'for it is Mr. Clinton who will have to relieve her at the finish.'

With these words we proceeded to the birching-room, which it appears had been furnished by these professors of flagellation with a nicety of detail and an eye to everything accessory to the art that was calculated to inspire a neophyte like myself with the utmost astonishment.

On a framework of green velvet was a soft down bed, and reclined on this length was the blushing Lucy.

Large bands of velvet, securely buckled at the sides, held her in position, while her legs, brought well together and fastened in the same way, slightly elevated her soft shapely arse.

The elevation was further aided by an extra cushion, which had been judiciously placed under the lower portion of her belly.

Monsignor bent over her and whispered a few soothing words into her ear, but she only buried her delicate head deeper into the down of the bed, while the reverend Father proceeded to analyse the points of her arse.

CHAPTER 8

THE EXPERIMENT PROCEEDS

Having all of them felt her arse in turn, pinching it as though to test its condition, much as a connoisseur in horseflesh would walk around an animal he was about to buy, Monsignor at length said 'What a superb picture.' His eyes were nearly bursting from their sockets. 'You must really excuse me, gentlemen, but my feelings overcome me,' and taking his comely prick out of his breeches, he deliberately walked up to Madeline, and before that fair damsel had guessed his intentions, he had thrown her down on the companion couch to Lucy's and had fucked her heart out in a shorter space of time than it takes me to write it.

To witness this was unutterably maddening. I scarcely knew what to be at; my heart beat wildly, and I should then and there have put myself into Lucy had I not been restrained by Father Boniface who, arch-vagabond that he was, took the whole business as a matter of course and merely observed to Monsignor that it would be as well to get it over as soon as possible, since Mr. Clinton was in a devil of a hurry.

Poor Lucy was deriving some consolation from Dr Price in the shape of a few drops of Pinero Balsam in champagne, while as for De Vaux, he was groaning audibly, and when the worthy Father Peter came to the short strokes De Vaux's chordee became so unbearable that he ran violently out into Monsignor's bedroom, as he afterwards informed me, to bathe his balls in ice water.

To me there was something rather low and shocking in a fuck before witnesses, but that is a squeamishness that I have long since got the better of.

Madeline, having wiped Monsignor's prick with a piece of mousseline de laine, a secret known only to the sybarite in love's perfect secrets, retired, presumably to syringe her fanny, and Monsignor buttoned up and approached his self-imposed task.

Taking off his coat he turned up his short cuffs and, Boniface handing him the birch rods, the bum-warming began.

At the first keen swish poor Lucy shrieked out, but before

half a dozen had descended with a quick smacking sound which betokens that there is no lack of elbow grease in the application, her groans subsided, and she spoke in a quick strained voice, begging for mercy.

'For the love of God,' she said, 'do not, pray do not lay it on so strong.'

By this time her lovely arse had assumed a flushed, vermilion tinge, which appeared to darken with every stroke, and at this point Dr Price interposed.

'Enough, Monsignor, now my duty begins.' And quick as thought he placed upon her bottom a piece of linen, which was smeared with an unguent, and stuck it at the sides with a small modicum of tar plaster to prevent it from coming off.

'Oh!' cried Lucy, 'I feel so funny. Oh! Mr. Clinton, if you are mere, pray relieve me, and make haste.'

In an instant my trousers were down, the straps were unbuckled, and Lucy was gently turned over on her back.

I saw a delicate bush of curly hair, a pair of glorious thighs, and the sight impelled me to thrust my prick into that divine Eden I had visited but a short time before with an ardour that for a man who had lived a fairly knockabout life was inexplicable.

I had scarcely got it thoroughly planted, and had certainly not made a dozen well-sustained though rapid strokes, before the gush of sperm which she emitted drew me at the same instant, and I must own that I actually thought the end of the world had come.

'Now,' said Dr Price, rapidly writing in his pocket-book, 'you see that my theory was correct. Here is a maid who has never known a man and she spends within ten seconds of the entrance being effected. Do you suppose that without the birching she could have performed such a miracle?'

'Yes,' I said, 'I do, and I can prove that all your surmises are but conjecture, and that even your conjecture is based upon a fallacy.'

'Bravo,' said Father Peter, 'I like to see Price fairly collared. Nothing flabbergasts him like facts. Dear me, how damnation slangy I am getting tonight. Lucy, dear, don't stand shivering mere, slip on your things and join Madeline in my snuggery; we shall all be mere presently. Go on, Clinton.'

'Well,' I said, 'it is easy enough to refute the learned doctor. In the first place Lucy was not a maid.'

'That be damned for a tale,' said Fattier Boniface. 'I got her mother to let me examine her myself last night while she was asleep, previous to handing over the hundred pounds.'

'Yes, that I can verify,' said Monsignor, 'though I must admit that you have a prick like a kitchen poker, for you got into her as easy as though she'd been on a Regent Street round for twenty years.'

'I will bet anyone here fifty to one,' I said, quietly taking out my pocket-book, 'that she was not a maid before I poked her just now.'

'Done,' said the doctor who, upon receiving a knowing wink from Father Peter, felt sure he was going to bag two ponies, 'and now how are we to prove it?'

'Ah, that will be difficult,' said Monsignor.

'Not at all,' I observed, 'let the young lady be sent for and questioned on the spot where you assume she was first deflowered of her virginity.'

'Yes, that's fair,' said De Vaux, and accordingly he called her in.

'My dear Lucy,' said Monsignor, 'I wish you to tell me the truth in answer to a particular question I am about to put to you.'

'I certainly will,' said Lucy, 'for God knows I have literally nothing now to conceal from you.'

'Well, that's not bad for a double entente,' said the Father, laughing, 'but now tell us candidly, before Mr. Clinton was intimate with you in our presence just now, had you ever before had a similar experience?'

'Once,' said Lucy, simpering and examining the pattern of the carpet.

'Good God,' said the astonished churchman, as with deathlike silence he waited for an answer to his next question-'When was it and with whom?'

'With Mr. Clinton himself, in the drawing-room here, about an hour ago.'

I refused the money of course, but had the laugh on all of them, and as we rolled home to De Vaux's chambers in a hansom about an hour later I could not help admitting to him that I considered the evening we had passed through the most agreeable I had ever known.

'You will soon forget it in the midst of other pleasures.'

'Never,' I said. 'If Calais was graven on Mary's heart, I am quite sure that this date will be found inscribed on mine if ever they should hold an inquest upon my remains.'

CHAPTER 9

A BACHELOR'S SUPPER PARTY

Having become a frequent visitor at The Priory, the name Monsignor's hospitable mansion was generally known by, I had numberless opportunities for fucking Lucy, Madeline and two of the domestics, but somehow I never properly took to flagellation in its true sense.

There was a housemaid of Monsignor's, a pretty and intelligent girl called Martha, the sight of whose large, fleshy bum, with an outline which would have crushed Hogarth's line of beauty out of time, used to excite me beyond measure, but I was not an enthusiast, and when Monsignor recognised this, and found that as a birch performer I laid it on far too sparingly, his invitations were less pressing, and gradually my visits became few and far between.

De Vaux, on the other hand, had become a qualified practitioner, and would dilate for hours on the celestial pleasures to be derived from skilful bum-scoring, in fact, so perfect a disciple of Monsignor's did he get to be that the pupil in some peculiar phases has outstripped the master, and his work now in the press, entitled The Glory of the Birch, or Heaven on Earth, may fairly claim, from an original point of view, to be catalogued with the more abstruse volumes penned by the Fathers, and collated and enlarged by Messrs Peter, Price and Boniface upon the same subject.

As I stated before, I could not enter so thoroughly into the felicity of birching. I saw that, physically speaking, it was productive of forced emission, but I preferred cunt moreau naturel. The easy transition from a kiss to a feel, from a feel to a finger frig, and eventually by a more natural sequence to a gentle insertion of the jock, were a series of gradations more suited to my unimaginative temperament, and I, therefore, to quote the regretful valediction of De Vaux, relapsed into that condition of Paphian barbarism in which he found me.

But I was by no means idle. My income, which was nearly?

7,000 per annum, was utilised in one direction only, and as you shall hear, I employed it judiciously in the gratification of my taste.

In the next suite of chambers to mine lived a young barrister, Sydney Mitchell, a daredevil dog, and one whose penchant for the fair sex was only equalled by his impecuniosity, for he was one of that many-headed legion who are known as briefless.

I had occasionally, when he had been pounced upon by a bailiff, which occurred on an average of about once a month, rescued him by a small advance, which he had gratefully repaid by keeping me company in my lonely rooms, drinking my claret and smoking my best Havanas.

But this was to me sufficient repayment, for Sydney had an inexhaustible store of comic anecdotes, and his smartly told stories were always so happily related that they never offended the ear, while they did not fail to tickle the erective organs.

One morning Sydney came to me in a devil of a stew.

'My very dear Clinton,' he said, 'I'm in a hell of a scrape again; can you help me out of it?'

'Is it much?' I said, remembering that I had paid?25 for him a few days before.

'Listen, and you may judge for yourself. I was at my Buffalo lodge last night, got drunk, and invited about half a dozen fellows to my chambers this evening to dinner.'

'Well,' I remarked, 'there's nothing very dreadful about that.'

'Yes, there is, for I have to appear as substitute for a chum on the Queen's Bench in an hour, and my wig is at the dresser's, who won't part with it until I've paid up what I owe, which will swallow up every penny I had intended for the dinner.'

'Oh, that's easily got over,' I said. 'Ask them to dine here instead, say you quite forgot you were engaged to me, and that I won't let you off, but desire they accompany you.'

'I'm your eternal debtor once more,' cried Sydney, and he rushed off to plead as happy as a butterfly.

I ordered a slap-up dinner for eight from the neighbouring restaurant, and as my 'Inn dinners' were well known by repute, not one of the invites was missing.

We had a capital dinner, and as Sydney's companions were a jolly set, I made up my mind for a glorious evening. Little did I know then how much more glorious it was to wind up than ever I had anticipated.

When the cigars and the port came on, and the meeting was beginning to assume a rather uproarious character, Sydney proposed that his friend Wheeler should oblige with a song, and after that gentleman had enquired whether my fastidiousness would be shocked at anything ultra drawing-room, and had been assured that nothing would give me greater pleasure, he began in a rich clear voice the following:

As Mary, dear Mary, one day was a-lying, As Mary, sweet Mary, one day was a-lying, She spotted her John, at the door he was spying, With his tol de riddle, tol de riddle, lol de rol lay.

And then came the chorus, rolled out by the whole company, for the refrain was so catching that I found myself unconsciously joining in withHis tol de riddle, tol de riddle, lol de rol lay.

Oh Johnny, dear Johnny, now do not come to me, Oh Johnny, pray Johnny, oh do not come to me, Or else I'm quite certain that you will undo me, With your tol de riddle, tol de riddle, lol de rol lay.

ChorusWith your tol de riddle, etc.

But Johnny, dear Johnny, not liking to look shady, But Johnny, sweet Johnny, not liking to seem shady, Why he downed with his breeches and treated his lad To his tol de riddle, tol de riddle, lol de rol lay.

ChorusWith your tol de riddle, etc.

Oh, Johnny, dear Johnny, you'll make me cry murder.

Oh, Johnny, pray cease this, you'll make me scream murder.

But she soon changed her note, and she murmured 'in further'

With your tol de riddle, tol de riddle, lol de rol lay.

Chorus – With your tol de riddle, etc.

Now Mary, dear Mary, grew fatter and fatter, Now Mary's, sweet Mary's plump belly grew fatter, Which plainly did prove that her John had been at her, With his tol de riddle, tol de riddle, lol de rol lay.

Chorus With your tol de riddle, etc.
MORAL

Now all you young ladies take warning had better, Now amorous damsels take warning you'd better, When you treat John make him wear a French letter.

On his tol de riddle, tol de riddle, lol de rol lay.

The singing of this song, which I was assured was quite original, was greeted with loud plaudits, then one of the young gentlemen volunteered a recitation, which ran as follows:

On the banks of a silvery river,
A youth and a maiden reclined;

The youth could be scarce twenty summers, The maiden some two years behind.

Full up and a neck well developed,
That youth's ardent nature bespoke,
And he gazed on that virtuous maiden
With a look she could hardly mistake.
But the innocent glance of that virgin
Betokened that no guile she knew,

Though he begged in bold tones of entreaty, She still wouldn't take up the cue.

He kissed her and prayed and beseeched her, No answer received in reply, Till his fingers were placed on her bosom, And he crossed his leg over her thigh.

Then she said, 'I can never, no never,
Consent to such deeds until wed;
You may try though the digital process,'
That maiden so virtuous said.

And he drew her still closer and closer, His hand quick placed under her clothes, And her clitoris youthful he tickled, Till that maiden excited arose.

'Fuck me now, dear, oh, fuck me,' she shouted, 'Fuck me now, fuck me now, or I die.'

'I can't, I have spent in my breeches,'
Was that youth's disappointing reply.

Monsignor Peter had, after an infinite amount of persuasion, given me the address where Pinero Balsam was to be obtained, and I had laid in a decent stock of it, for though each small bottle cost a sovereign, I felt morally sure that it was the nearest approximation to the mythical elixir vitae of the ancients that we moderns had invented. Some of this I had secretly dropped into the port wine, and the effect upon my guests had already become very pronounced.

'I say, Clinton,' said the Junior of the party, who had only 'passed' a month before, and who might be just turned twenty, 'your dinner was splendid, your tipple has a bouquet such as my inexperience has never suggested. Have you anything in the shape of petticoats about half so good? If so, give me a look in.'

The youth was rapidly getting maudlin and randy; just then came a faint rap at the door. It was the old woman who swept and garnished the 'diggings'.

'I thought I might find Mr. Mitchell here, sir,' she said apologetically, 'here's a telegram come for him.' And curtsying, the old girl vanished, glad to escape the fumes of wine and weed which must have nearly choked her.

'No bad news, I hope,' I said.

'Not at all,' said Sydney. 'What's the time?'

'Nearly 8.30,' I replied, consulting my chronometer.

'Then I shall have to leave you fellows at nine; my married sister Fanny arrives at Euston from the north on the 9.30.'

'What a pity!' said the callow Junior, 'if it were a sweetheart now one might be overjoyed at your good fortune-but a sister!'

'Is it the handsome one?' put in Wheeler.

'Yes,' said Sydney, showing us the face in a locket, the only piece of jewellery he boasted.

There was a silence as all clustered around the likeness.

'By Jove,' said Tom Mallow, the roue of the party, 'if I had a sister like that I should go clean staring mad to think she wasn't some other fellow's sister, so that I might have a fair and reasonable chance.'

I said nothing, but I fell in love with that face to such an extent that I felt there was nothing I would not do to possess the owner.

I, of course, presented a calm exterior, and under the guise of a host who knew his duty, plied them with a rare old port, and proposed toast after toast and health after health, until I had the satisfaction of seeing in less than three-quarters of an hour, every member of the crew so dead drunk that I felt I could afford to leave the chambers without any fear of a mishap; then rolling the recumbent Sydney over, for he was extended prone upon the hearth-rug, I subtracted the wire from his pocket and saw that his sister's name was Lady Fanny Twisser.

'Oh,' I said, a light breaking in upon me, 'this then is the girl Sydney's plotting mother married to a rich baronet old enough to be her grandfather; this doubles my chances,' and locking the door I made my way into the street. It was 9.19, and I was a mile and a quarter from the station.

'Hansom!'

'Yes, sir.'

'A guinea if you can drive me to Euston Station in ten minutes.'

That man earned his guinea.

CHAPTER 10

THE EFFECTS OF SHELLFISH

From the booking office I emerged on to the arrival platform, and hailing a superior-looking porter, placed a sovereign in his hand, whispering in his ear 'The train coming in the distance contains a Lady Twisser; engage a good cab, put all her luggage on it, and if I should happen to miss the lady, as I might do in this crowd, conduct me to her.'

He obeyed my instructions au pied de la lettre, and in less than two minutes I was shaking hands on the strength of a self-introduction with Lady Fanny.

I explained that her brother was engaged in consultation with a senior counsel at the bar, and that, had it not been a very important case, he would have met her in person, but my instructions were that she was to come to his chambers, where he would probably be by the time we arrived.

Lady Fanny's portrait had by no means exaggerated her loveliness.

A stately Grecian nose and finely cut lips suggested to me that she was a mare that might shy, but then her soft, brown, dreamy eyes told a sweeter tale, and I leaned back in the cab and almost wished I had not touched the Pinero cordial, for I was in momentary fear of spending in my trousers.

'This, I think, is your first visit to London.'

'Scarcely,' she replied, in a voice whose gentle music made my heart bound, 'I came up with my husband six months ago to be "presented, but we only stayed the day.'

'London is a splendid city,' I rejoined, 'so full of life and gaiety, and the shops and bazaars are always replete with every knick-knack; for ladies it must seem a veritable paradise.'

Lady Fanny only sighed, which I thought strange, but before my cogitations could take form we were at my chambers.

'Had not my boxes better be sent to some hotel?' said Lady Fanny. 'I am, of course, only going to make a call here.'

'Yes,' I returned, 'that is all arranged,' and tipping the

cabman handsomely, I directed him to take them to a quiet hotel in Norfolk Street, Strand, and conducted her ladyship to her brother's rooms.

Here I left her for a few moments to see after my drunken guests, but found them all snoring peacefully, some on the floor, others on chairs and sofas, but all evidently settled for the night.

After knocking at Sydney's door I again entered his sitting-room, but found it empty.

Damn it, I thought to myself, the bird hasn't flown, I hope.

My ears were at this moment saluted with the gurgling which signalled that her ladyship was relieving herself in the adjoining apartment, and I quietly sat down and awaited her return.

On seeing me she started and turned as red as a full-blown peony, the flower being a simile suggested by the situation, and said, 'I had no idea, Mr. Clinton, that-'

'Pray, Lady Fanny, do not mention it; I know exactly what you were about to say.'

'Indeed?'

'Yes, you as a matter of fact didn't know what to say, because you thought I heard you-a-hem-in the next room-but, my dear Lady Fanny, in London we are not so particular as the hoydenish country folks, and as an old friend of your brother's you will pardon my saying that I do not think you have treated me overly well.' 'Treated you- really, Mr. Clinton, you amaze me; pray what have I done?'

'Rather, my dear Lady Fanny, what have you left undone.'

'Nothing, I hope,' she said hastily, looking down as though she expected to see a petticoat or a garter falling off.

'No, I don't mean anything like that,' I said, coming closer to her, until the flame which shot from my eyes appeared to terrify her, and she moved towards the bedroom, as if to take refuge there.

Now this was the very height of my ambition; I knew once in that apartment all struggles and cries would be of little avail, for the walls were thick, the windows high, and there was no other door save the one she was gradually backing into.

'What does this conduct mean, Mr. Clinton?' said the lovely

girl. 'I surely am in my brother's chambers, and with his friend, for he has often written and told me of your kindness to him. You are not an impostor, one of those dreadful men of whom one reads in romances, who would harm a woman?'

'No,' I said. 'Lady Fanny, do not mistake the ardour of devotion for any sinister motive, but sit down, after your fatiguing journey, while I order in some refreshment.'

Doubly locking the door, on the principle of safe bind, safe find, I gave an order to the restaurateur around the corner which astonished that gentleman, and in less than ten minutes I had overcome Fanny's scruples, got her to take off her moire mantle and coquettish bonnet, and had placed before her a bijou supper in five courses such as I knew would make a country demoiselle open her eyes.

'Good gracious me,' said Lady Fanny, 'does my brother always live like this? If so, I am not at all surprised at his frequent requisitions on my purse.'

'Yes,' I said nonchalantly, 'this is generally our supper. Permit me.' And I poured out a glass of champagne, taking care, however, that six drops of Pinero had been placed in the glass.

CHAPTER 11

A DISAPPOINTED WIFE'S FIRST TASTE OF BLISS

The effect was really magical, for her conversation, hitherto so constrained, became gay and lively, and as this vivacity added to her other charms, I grew more and more enamoured of her.

What capital oysters these are,' she said, swallowing her ninth 'native'. *Yes,' I said, 'in your Cheshire home you would find it difficult to procure such real beauties.'

We should, indeed,' she replied, 'and for the matter of that it is perhaps better that shellfish are so scarce with us,' and she heaved another sigh.

This beautiful woman is decidedly a conundrum, I thought, but determined to probe the puzzle, I enquired the meaning of her last remark.

She blushed and simpered, then fixing her eyes on her plate said, 'I have always understood that shellfish are exciting, and stimulate the passions.'

That is perfectly correct,' I retorted, 'and therefore all the more reason why a married lady should patronise them.'

She sighed again, and then at last I guessed the reason.

Fool that I was not to have divined it before this time. Hope now was succeeded by certainty.

After disposing of some chicken and another glass of champagne, into which I had dropped some more balsam, she sank back into the armchair and murmured'How long do you think my brother's consultation is likely to last?'

'Pray heaven,' I ejaculated fervently, 'that it may last all the night through.'

'Why do you say that, Mr. Clinton?'

'Because to see you and to listen to your voice is ravishing delight, which to dispel would seem to me the precursor of death.' And I flung myself upon my knees before her, and seizing her hand pressed it to my lips and covered it with burning kisses.

She gently tried to withdraw it, and pointing to her wedding ring, said'Dear Mr. Clinton, I am a wife, have pity on me, I am but a weak woman and-'

But I caught her in my arms, and stifled the rest of the sentence with a long and ardent embrace, which, repulsed at first, was at length returned.

Two seconds afterwards, my finger had softly insinuated itself into her willing cunt, and as it encountered the clitoris I found that it was as stiff as my own penis, which was now at the bursting point.

'Oh, Mr. Clinton, for God's sake forbear. If my brother should come in there would be blood spilled, I should be lost.'

'Fear nothing, my darling,' I said, rubbing her vagina with the point of my finger, and feeling the beginning of the pearly trickle exuding all over my hand.

'Come this way.' And leading her ladyship by the hand, never, however, leaving hold of her sweet cunt the while, I placed her on her own brother's bed, and, oh, how can I write further, since to say that she was superb is but faintly to describe the joy I felt as straightening my throbbing prick, I gently slipped it into her.

She gave one loud sigh, then lifted her strong country arse so that I plunged in up to the hilt. At each thrust I gave her ladyship she responded with a promptitude which showed how fresh and spunky her vigorous constitution was.

'Go on, my own precious,' she whispered, as I put my tongue into her panting hot mouth. 'Faster, for Christ's sake, faster.'

And as she said the words I shot into her a discharge which must have clean emptied my cods, for although Fanny still faintly struggled to elicit some more, the last lingering spark of vitality appeared to have flown from me.

I did not seem to have even the strength left to take it out, but lay there on her rounded breasts (for she had undone her clothes before commencing), supine and nerveless.

'Do try again, love,' she murmured, toying with my hair. 'You will never guess, dear Mr. Clinton, what this has been to me, my old husband never did such a thing, he always uses a beastly machine, shaped like that which is in me now, but made of gutta-percha, and filled with warm oil and milk.'

'You mean a dildo, dear?'

'I have never heard its name,' said Fanny, 'but it is nothing near so nice as this dear sweet thing of yours. Oh! I never knew what real happiness was before; could you manage it once more?' And again her ladyship wriggled her bottom.

In my waistcoat pocket I had a petite flask of Pinero.

I took this out and, removing the stopper, drank about half a teaspoonful; the result was electrical. Drawing my prick nearly out of my lady's passage, I found it swelling again; and just giving the potent charm time to work, I softly began once more.

It may almost seem romantic, but I can assure my readers that the second fuck was more enjoyable than the first.

For having made coition a long study, I have always found that, given a cool brain, I can get more pleasure out of a slow connection than a gallopade, where the excitement gets the business over before you can absolutely realise the details.

I revel in slow friction, gradually warming up to fever heat, and quite agree with that exquisite stanza of the immortal native of Natal – Who was poking a Hottentot gal, and who, upon being remonstrated with thusSaid she, 'Oh! you sluggard,' replied most correctly'You be buggered, I like fucking slow, and I shall.'

To resume. We both seemed to be so au courant of each other's little ways and modes of action as though we had mutually performed the 'fandango de pokum' for years, instead of only a few short minutes.

Presently, to vary the bliss, and to give her ladyship a few wrinkles, I suggested her mounting me, ala St. George.

But she begged of me not to take it out, and on my assuring her that was by no means a necessary concomitant, she agreed.

I have always been distinguished as being particularly au fait with the St George, so I managed to roll over very gradually, first one leg and then the other, till I had got Fanny fairly planted on top of me.

But I had gauged her ladyship's cunt power at too low an estimate, for she no sooner found herself mistress of the situation than she took in the position at a glance, and ravished me with such terrible lunges that I fairly cried a 'go'.

But nothing daunted, Fanny held on, and I stood no more

chance of getting my poor used-up 'torch' out of her vagina than if it had been wedged into a vice.

At last I felt the hot crane de la creme pouring down over my balls, and with a last despairing gasp of mingled pleasure and regret to think she could hold out no longer, Fanny once more sank into my arms about as thoroughly spent as a woman should be who has been most damnably twice fucked in a quarter of an hour.

Hastily putting on her things, and making herself shipshape, she drove with me to the hotel, where her boxes had arrived safely, and in the morning I informed her brother, as I had previously arranged with Fanny, that she had sent a messenger to his chambers overnight, saying where she was to be found.

I also told him how I had excused him in a return message by the hotel porter, and his gratitude to me knew no bounds.

I deemed it prudent not to see her ladyship during her stay in town, though she sent me three pressing letters, but I feared we should be bowled out, and wrote her so.

Twelve months after this I heard she had separated from her husband, having presented him, nine months from that blissful evening, with a son and heir, which the old man, not believing in miracles, could scarcely altogether credit the dildo with.

CHAPTER 12

THE INFLUENCE OF FINERY

Now my next essay was of a totally different character, and may, perhaps, be stigmatised by the fastidious reader as an escapade, degrading to one whose last liaison had been with the wife of a baronet, but to tell the truth, and judging cunt from a strictly philosophical standpoint, there is so little difference between a chambermaid and a countess, that it would take a very astute individual indeed to define it. It is, perhaps, true, that the countess's opening may be, by frequent ablutions, kept sweeter, and the frangipani on her ladyship's fine cambric chemisette may possibly make the entrance more odoriferous for a tongue lick, but Dr Johnson's admirable impromptu definition will apply to the vagina of a Malayan or a Chinese girl equally with that of our own countrywomen. He said, if you remember, on the occasion when poor Oliver Goldsmith was troubled with the venereal, and came to him for sympathy'Cunt, and what of it?

A nasty, slimy, slobbery slit,

Half an inch between arse and it;

If the bridge were to break, y'd would be covered with – '

I have already in the course of this narrative mentioned the duenna who cleaned my chambers. She was a cast-off mistress of one of the old sergeants of the Inn, who had procured her this situation for life, and supplemented it with a small allowance, which enabled her to live in comparative comfort.

Two of her bastard daughters were married, and a younger one, the pretty one as she called her, had just returned home from boarding school, whither the old woman by dint of careful frugality had managed to send her.

She was barely turned sixteen, as upright as a dart, had a fine full face, with plenty of colour in it, and a form so shapely that I scarcely gave credence to the mother's statement that she was only sixteen. The old woman was very garrulous, annoyingly so sometimes, but on the subject of her darling daughter I used to let her tongue run on till further orders.

'She's a fine, strapping wench, sir, just the kind of girl I was at her age, though I think if anything she's a trifle more plump than I was.'

'Yes, by God, and so should I,' was my involuntary exclamation, as I looked at the aged frump's wizened features.

'I don't know what I shall do with her,' muttered her mother. 'I shall have to send her to service; this place won't keep two of us, and not only that, sir, I've been thinking that it's hardly the thing for a giddy girl like her to be brought into contact with gentlemen like you.'

Of course the mother was thinking of her own youthful transgressions with the sergeant, so I merely remarked that I was surprised such thoughts should run in her head, but I inwardly resolved that come what might I would see if a girl of sixteen with such a full fleshy face had got a cunt to match.

Noticing that the daughter was fond of dress, I bought a small parcel of ribbons one day at the draper's, and had them addressed to her without saying a word as to my having sent them.

The following morning I met her on the stairs, gaily decked out, and I asked her where she was going.

'Only for a walk in this silly old inn,' she replied. 'I have a beau, sir, an unknown beau, who has sent me all these beautiful ribbons, and a lot more besides, and I thought by going out he might see that I had appreciated his gift, that is if he were watching for me,' she added, with an arch smile.

'That's right, my girl, perhaps he will send you something else; by the way, what is your name?'

'Gerty,' said the young lady, smiling.

'Well, Gerty, you'll excuse my saying so, but that splendid ribbon with which you have decorated your hat, makes the hat look quite shabby.'

'Alas! sir, I know it, but Mother is poor, and I can't afford to buy another one just yet.'

'If you'd promise not to tell your mother-promise me sacredly not on any account to tell her-I will take you to a shop where I saw a lovely one yesterday that would suit your style admirably, and I shall be only too happy to purchase it for you.'

'Oh! sir, you are very kind, but I could not impose-'

'Tut, child, don't speak like that, but go out into the street and walk to the corner of Great Turnstile, and I will join you in three minutes.'

Of course I did this to avoid observation. Presently I went out myself, and took her to the very draper's where I had bought the ribbon.

'Good-morning, sir, I have now got that particular shade of ribbon you wanted yesterday.'

The cat was out of the bag; Gerty glanced quickly up at me, and I saw I was discovered.

'So you are the unknown beau,' she whispered, 'well, I am surprised.'

'And, I hope, pleased, too, Gerty?'

'Well, I hardly know,' she said, 'but what about the hat?'

To cut a long story short I rigged her up from top to toe, and before I left the shop I had expended nearly?20 on her.

'How on earth am I to account for having this to Mother?'

'We'll have it sent like the ribbons, and, of course, you can't form a guess where it came from. The shop people must put no address inside.' And giving all the necessary instructions, I shook hands with Gertrude and bade her good-morning.

In the evening a gentle tap at my door ushered in the young lady herself, who, closing it softly after her, said 'Those things have come, sir, and Mother went on like anything, but I vowed I didn't know who had sent 'em, so she told me in that case I'd better thank God, and say no more about it.'

'Then it's all right,' I said, looking intently at her large, rounded bust, which, confined as it was by a tightly-fitting dress, showed itself to singular advantage.

'I'm afraid, sir,' she said, 'that I didn't thank you sufficiently this morning, and so I thought as mother has gone down to Peckham to see her brother, I'd call in and do it now.'

'My dear Gertrude,' I said, 'there's only one way of showing your gratitude to me, and that way you are as yet I fear too young to understand. Come here, my dear.'

I was sitting by a blazing coal fire, and although I had not lit the gas the light was ample; she stepped forward and seemed, as I thought, rather timorous in her manner.

'My dear Gerty,' I said, placing my arm around her waist, 'you are heartily welcome to what my poor purse can afford. As for those pretty matters I purchased today, one kiss from those pouting lips will repay me a thousandfold.' And so saying I lifted her on to my knee and kissed her repeatedly.

At first she tried to disengage herself, but soon I found my caresses were not unwelcome. Presently I began undoing the buttons of her frock, and although she fought against it at first, she gradually allowed herself to be convinced, and as her swelling bubs disclosed themselves to my view I felt transported.

'Oh! Mr. Clinton, you will ruin me, I'm sure you will. Pray stop where you are, and do not go any further.'

Her beautiful little nipples, as the firelight threw them into relief on her lily-white breasts, looked like a pair of twin cherries, and before she could prevent me, my mouth had fastened on one, and I sucked it avidly.

'Oh! Mr. Clinton, I shall faint. Do let me go. I never felt anything like this in my life.'

'My darling,' I said, suddenly placing my prick in her hand, 'did you ever feel anything like that?'

Her thumb and fingers clutched it with a nervous clasp, and I felt that her hands were moist with the hot dew of feverish perspiration. Before, however, I could prevent her, or, indeed, fathom her motives, she had slid from my grasp, and was kneeling on the floor between my extended legs.

'What is the matter, Gerty dear?' I said.

I got no answer, but the hand which still held my penis was brought softly forward, her mouth opened, and drawing back my foreskin, she tongued me with a sweet suck that almost drove me frantic.

For at least two minutes I lay back in the armchair, my brain in a delirium of delight, until, unable to bear it any longer, for she had begun to rack me off, I got my prick away, pushed back the armchair, and with mad, and, I may add, stupid haste, broke her maidenhead, and spent in her at the same instant with such force that for the moment I expected (contrary to all anatomical knowledge) to see the sperm spurting out of her mouth.

It would be unjust to Gertrude were I to accuse her of want of reciprocity, for my hearth-rug gave ample good proof that she was by no means wanting in juice, since to say it was swamped would be but mildly to describe its condition.

Hardly had Gertrude wiped out her fanny, and just as I was in the act of pouring her out a glass of brandy and water, to prevent the reaction which in a maid so young might, I thought, possibly set in, when, without announcing her entrance, the mother rushed into the room like a tigress. She had returned to fetch her latchkey.

'So this is what I brought you up for like a lady, is it,' she began; 'and this is the conduct of a gentleman that I thought was a real gentleman. Don't deny it, you brazen bitch,' she continued, seeing that Gertrude was about to try a lame explanation, for she was quick-witted enough. 'I've got a nose of my own, and if ever there was a maidenhead cooked it's been done in this room since I've been out. Why, even the staircase smells fishy. I discard you forever. Perhaps the gentleman,' laying a sneering stress on the word, 'now that he's ruined you, will keep you.' And she bounced out of the room.

I took the old woman at her word, and rented a little cottage at Kew, where I kept Gerty in style for about three months, and should have done so to the end of the chapter if I had not caught her one Saturday afternoon in flagrante delicto with one of the leading members of the London Rowing Club; so I gave her a cheque for ?100, and she started as a dressmaker, or something of the kind, at which business she has I understand done very well.

CHAPTER 13

A PARAGON OF VIRTUE

One morning, as the summer was waning, and August warned us to flee from town, De Vaux called upon me at my new chambers (for prudence had suggested my removal from my late quarters) and found me dozing over a prime Cabana, and the latest chic book from Mr. -, the renowned smut purveyor.

'Glad to see you,' said De Vaux. 'My friend Leveson has asked me down to Oatlands Hall for a week's shooting, and wishes me to bring a friend. Will you come?'

'Is there anything hot and hollow about,' I asked, 'for to tell you the truth, my boy, knocking over the grouse is a very pleasant occupation, but unless there is some sport of another kind on as well, the game is not worth the candle.'

'Clinton, you are incorrigible. I never remember having met such an incurable cunt-hunter in my life. Well, there may be some stray stuff dropping in while we are there, but I warn you not to try it with Mrs. Leveson, for though she might give you the idea at a first glance that she was fast and frivolous, she's in reality as true as steel to her husband, and I would not give a brass farthing for the chance of the veriest Adonis that ever stood in a pair of patent leather boots.'

'I should immensely like to have a slap at this dreadful Diana of yours, De Vaux. Is she a beauty?'

De Vaux sighed heavily.

'I was hard hit myself in that quarter once,' he said, 'but it was no go. Her eyes are wandering orbs, like a gypsy's. She has the finest set of teeth I ever saw in my life, and a form, well-I'd rather not go into it, for it upsets me.'

'I'd rather go into it, for my part,' I said, laughing. 'Why, you're a very Strephon, De Vaux, in your poetic keep-at-a-distance style of admiring this divinity. Did you seriously try it on, now, left no stone unturned, eh?'

'I did, indeed,' said De Vaux, 'both before and after she was married, but it was love's labour lost. I got my hand on her leg once, and she froze me with a few curt words, and wound up by telling me if I did not instantly go back to town, and foist some lying excuse on Leveson for going, she would expose me mercilessly, and by God, Clinton, I am sufficiently learned in womankind to know when they mean a thing and when they do not.'

'Really, I must see this paragon of yours, De Vaux. The more obstacles there are in me way, the better a Philosopher in Cunt enjoys it'

'You can come with me and welcome, Clinton, but I tell you candidly, Mrs. Leveson is beyond your reach or that of any other man. She is simply ice.'

'But, my dear De Vaux, ice can be made to thaw!'

'Not the ice of the poles.'

'Yes, even that, if you apply sufficient heat. Bah! my friend, I'll wager you twelve dozen of my finest Chateau Margaux to that emerald pin you wear, for which I have often longed, that I will fuck your pearl of chastity before this day week.'

The bet was instantly accepted; although I had previously offered him?50 for his pin and he had refused to part with it, still he felt no danger in the present instance, and went home and probably drank in his imagination half of my wine in anticipation.

'Clinton my boy,' I said, apostrophising my prick as I got into bed that evening, 'if you don't disturb her ladyship's ice-bound repose before many nights have gone over your proud red head may you be damned to all eternity,' and, in response, my noble, and, I may add, learned friend, perked himself up straight, and though he didn't speak, his significant and conceited nod assured me that he at any rate had no misgivings.

CHAPTER 14

OTHER GAME PREFERRED TO GROUSE

We arrived at Oatlands Hall about five o'clock in the afternoon, after a delightful journey, for it was the 11th of August and the mellow corn just fully ripened for the sickle greeted our city-worn eyes all along the line. So really picturesque was the view that I lost several opportunities of getting well on with a buxom young chit who wanted fucking worse than anything in petticoats ever did between London and York.

De Vaux slept most of the way, and if without committing murder I could have got the girl's mother out of the carriage window, I should certainly have landed a slice of sixteen, for she could not have been over that age.

Leveson was a very jolly fellow, about thirty-eight or forty, and Airs Leveson, a really grand creature, was at least ten to twelve years his junior, but although De Vaux had prepared me for something above the ordinary, I must confess the reality far surpassed my expectations.

Figurez-vous, as our lively neighbours would put it, a sweet smiling Juno with an oval face, coloured prettily by nature's own palette, and a pair of finely arched eyebrows surrounding eyes so dazzling in their lustrous black that I fell a victim to the very first glance.

Poor De Vaux seemed half in doubt, half dread, for this was the first time he had seen her since the fiasco. She, however, stretched out her hand and welcomed him cordially.

We had a fine, old-fashioned country dinner, and then Mrs. Leveson proposed a stroll around the grounds. She took great pride in the garden and orchard, and the exquisite fascination of her manner as she described lucidly all the various differences between plants, shrubs, greenery, exotics, and all the thousand and one trifles that interest a botanical student showed me that she was no ordinary woman.

Again I was compelled to silent admiration when we walked through the stables, which Caligula's could scarcely have excelled for cleanliness, and as she patted the horses in their boxes I envied them, for they neighed and whinnied with delight at her very touch.

I was glad when she and her husband had gone into the house, and left De Vaux and me to finish our smoke alone.

'Well,' he said, 'what do you think of her?'

'Think of her,' I muttered, 'I'd rather not think of her, she has excited me to such an extent that if I don't get into something in the house I shall really have to go into the village and seek out an ordinary "pross".' "Well, my dear boy, then you'd better do that at once, for unless some of the chambermaids are amenable, I'm perfectly certain that you've no time to lose. You might as well dream of fucking the moon as Mrs. Leveson. She's quite as chaste and just as unattainable.'

'That be damned,' I said. De Vaux's constant reiteration of this Dulcinea's chastity was gall and wormwood to me.

We were the only guests who had arrived for the 12th, and as grouse shooting meant getting up at dawn, we had one rubber at whist, and retired to bed early.

On the first floor of this large old mansion there were at least a dozen rooms. My own bedroom door immediately faced our host and hostess's; De Vaux slept in the next room to mine.

'How frightfully hot it is,' said Leveson. 'I should say we're bound to have some rain.'

'I hope not,' I said, 'for it will spoil our morning, though this temperature is simply insufferable.' I had been all around the world in my father's yacht, and had spent a considerable time in the tropics, but never remembered such an intense dry heat.

Taking with me to bed a French novel I had picked out of the library shelves, and getting the servant to bring in a large glass of lemonade, I was soon asleep, in spite of the heat, though I had to forgo sheets, blanket and counterpane, and simply slept in my nightshirt.

In the grey of the morning I was aroused, and could scarcely believe my eyes. There was a young woman standing by the side of the bed, and I recognised her as the shapely lass who had taken my portmanteau upstairs the previous evening.

I have always had an unpleasant habit in my sleep of

twisting and turning until my shirt tucks up under my armpits. Thus it appeared that, as this hot night had proved no exception to the rule, Hannah, for such was the filly's name, had knocked at the door to awaken me, but receiving no response, and fearing she should get into trouble if I overslept myself, had opened the door, and the sight of my magnificent prick had simply transfixed her so that she stood there like one bewitched.

I rubbed my eyes once more, then sprang up, and before the girl could, like a frightened fawn, reach the door, I had gently but firmly closed it, and set my back against it.

'Oh! Mr. Clinton, missis would be so angry if she heard me in here.'

'Has your mistress been called yet?'

'No sir.'

'Have you aroused Mr. De Vaux?'

'Not yet.'

'Who knows then of your being here?'

'The cook, sir, and she's a spiteful old thing as hates gentlemen, because they don't never look at her.'

'Hannah,' I said, 'didn't I hear you called by that name last night?'

'Yes sir; please let me go downstairs.'

'Hannah, is there light enough for you to see this?' and I quietly raised my nightshirt.

'Oh, Mr. Clinton, how can you be so rude!'

'Now, look here, Hannah, we needn't mince words. Your mistress doesn't know of your being here, but if you cry out she's bound to know it, and of course you'll get sacked for being found in a gentleman's bedroom. I shan't be blamed for trying to get into a girl who actually comes to ask me for it.'

'But, my God, I haven't sir.'

'No, but don't you see that is what I should be obliged to say if any awkward questions were put to me.'

'Oh! please sir, I'll never come into your bedroom again, sir, indeed I won't.'

'My dear Hannah,' I said, 'I hope you will every night of my stay, but I must have my first taste now.'

With a sudden movement I caught her in my arms and

threw her down on the bed.

The silly stupid fool struggled with the strength of a giantess, and I saw that it was going to be a fair fight for it.

This is what I enjoy, provided the struggle is not too exhausting, and in this case it was fortunately only of sufficient duration to give the proper zest, for no sooner in the course of her efforts to keep my hand away from her fanny had her own touched the top of my splitting jock, than she was powerless as a kitten.

I will not dilate upon my fuck with Hannah, for she was in too frightened a state to give me much pleasure at that time.

I have, however, under more favourable conditions, since amused myself with her during a spare half-hour, and although her cunt has not got that tenacity of grip which distinguished Lady Fanny, for example, yet there was that general spunkiness about her final throw-off which places her in the front rank for one of her station of life.

Again to quote dear old Sam: 'A man's imagination is not so inflamed with a chambermaid as a countess,' and besides, Hannah was not a maid, the coachman having settled her hash about six months before.

CHAPTER 15

CHECKED AT FIRST

After our bout, Hannah kissed me and bolted off, and I drank a tumbler of water with a few drops of balsam in it and, feeling none the worse for my affaire par basard, at once joined the shooting party.

I did a fair share of bagging, though the birds were scarcely wild enough to suit my taste.

I hate the fashionable battue business of today, but do not mean to imply that it was anything like that, for I am speaking of more than twenty years ago, but still Leveson's keepers had fed them too well, and they scarcely rose to the tramp of a foot near their cover.

We returned to the hall for lunch, and Mrs. Leveson enquired as to the results of our morning's work. We told her it had been fair, but I half hinted at my preference for seeing a bit of the country, as I was a fickle sportsman, and one morning's shooting was enough for me. She, without a moment's hesitation, offered to become my cicerone and, procuring two horses from the stable, we sallied forth together.

'Now, you must be my mentor in everything, please, Mrs. Leveson,' I told her. 'I must admit to being dreadfully ignorant of country matters.'

We rode fully fifteen miles, and although I felt my way cautiously, I began to see there was an iron barrier between us which would probably prove impassable.

The instant there was the slightest hint or suggestion which implied a double entente her cheek flushed, and she looked fully in my face with her sparkling eyes, and a gaze of steady searching frankness as if to say, 'Do my ears deceive me, or are you trying to insult me?'

'Damn it,' I thought, 'James Clinton, you've met your match this time.' And a still small voice never left off whispering, 'See what the balsam will do, try a few drops of it.' But I never got the opportunity, and as we cantered down the broad gravel walk that led to the front lawn, she with her face flushed with the excitement of riding, mine flushed also, but with the excitement of a 'horn' which I now had the satisfaction of knowing could be relieved without quitting the mansion, De Vaux met us.

'Well,' he said in an undertone to me, after he had assisted Mrs. Leveson to dismount, 'how does the bet stand?'

'Blast the bet,' I said, 'I'll give you six dozen to let me off.'

He laughed and said he would take one hundred and forty-three bottles, and leave me the other to get drunk upon and drown my disappointment.

CHAPTER 16

FORTUNE FAVOURS THE BRAVE

Hannah did not come up to my room that night, though she had promised to; still the weather was again so damned hot that I was in one sense rather glad of it. About four a.m., however, she came up to call the indefatigable sportsmen, but Leveson had already risen, and had entered my room in his shirt and trousers, so that when Hannah gently opened my door she was petrified at finding her master there trying to persuade me to go with them.

'What the devil do you mean, you minx, by coming into a gentleman's room without knocking first?'

I immediately interposed, and told him what a sound sleeper I was, and spoke of the difficulty the girl had experienced the previous morning.

'Mr. De Vaux is up, so you needn't trouble to call him, and you needn't bring up any coffee to your mistress, for she's as sound asleep as a rock. So you won't come, Clinton?'

'Not this morning, old boy; I'm deuced tired and sleepy.'

Very well, then,' he said, 'I suppose we must manage without you.' And presently I heard both the noble sportsmen quietly taking their departure.

I at first tried to compose myself to sleep, but found it impossible, for my prick had become a cursed encumbrance. The advent of Hannah had excited it to start with, and now there was the tantalising fact that within a few yards of me was lying the lady of the mansion, yet, in respect to approachability, as far off as if she had been at the Antipodes.

Still the old proverb of 'faint heart never winning fair lady' came to my rescue, and I quietly arose and softly opened my door, just to see if there was a ghost of a chance.

As I previously mentioned, my room faced that of Mr. and Mrs. Leveson's. Judge then my delight when I saw that my host had actually, and I presumed by inadvertence, left his door ajar.

Stealthily and silently as a cat I crossed the corridor, scarcely daring to breathe, and pushing the door open, inch by inch, I put my head inside.

There, lying on the bed with nothing but a sheet to cover her splendid form, was the woman for whose possession I so madly longed, but the knowledge that her chastity was an insuperable bar to the ordinary preliminaries of a fair fuck suggested my attempting the siege in another fashion.

Stooping down and going on all fours, I approached the bedside, and gently lifting up one end of the sheet I revealed her naked form, for, like me, she had got her night-chemise rolled up as far as her titties. Her legs were lying temptingly open and, as little by little I worked myself under the sheet, my face drew nearer to the lovely little cunt whose pouting lips looked fit to be kissed.

Gradually, and without sufficient movement to alarm or even awaken my sleeping beauty, I got my head well between her legs.

She did move once, and passed her hand down over my head, murmuring the while – 'Oh George, wait until morning.' And as I remained perfectly quiet, she dozed off again.

Presently I got well into position, and putting out my tongue, gave the lips a gentle lick. I could feel that there was a slight tremor, but as that was only the natural effect of the electro biology, I knew that she was not yet awake.

Another lick, this time a trifle further in, and the next second I plunged my tongue far up, until it touched the clitoris. She was instantly awake.

'Oh George darling, it is years since you did this. Why, you dog, you haven't thought of such a thing since our honeymoon.'

I renewed my licking, thrusting her splendid thighs aside (though, in reality, there was no need to thrust, for she opened them as far as ever she could) until my tongue was in right up to the root, and I found from the rapid up and down movement of her bottom that, unless I speedily withdrew it, she would most certainly come.

In my excitement I muttered 'my darling', and she, hearing a strange voice, threw back the sheet, and I suppose looked down.

She must have seen at a glance that it was not her husband, for she put her hands on my head, and in a low voice, half anguish, half pleasure, said-'Oh, who are you? How could you?'

But the matter had gone too far now to be remedied, and she must have felt this, for the movement of her arse continued, and was getting more violent.

I could stand it no longer, so taking out my tongue, I looked up at her.

'I guessed it was you, Mr. Clinton. You are doing a very wicked thing, but I really must have it now, I can't wait,' and pulling me on to her, she guided my prick to the already well-greased hole, which was full of slobber from my own mouth, and with several quick movements, long thrusts, and about half a dozen wriggles, we both spent at the same moment.

I believe, had her husband come in at that instant, we could not possibly have disengaged ourselves from each other's arms, for we lay mere in a transport of bliss, and I could not help pluming myself on the admirable savoir-faire I had manifested in my management of the whole business.

'What on earth made you do this, Mr. Clinton?' said Mrs. Leveson, still holding me and keeping me in her, with her legs entwined around my backside, but blushing all the while.

'My darling,' I said, 'the moment I saw you I felt that if I had to commit a rape I should be obliged to enjoy you, though it cost me my liberty, or indeed, for the matter of that, my life.'

A light movement outside the door attracted our attention, and hiding me under the sheet, Mrs. Leveson enquired who was there; to this there was no response, and we breathed freely again.

'My darling,' said Mrs. Leveson, looking at me with beaming eyes, 'I am so delighted that although I know we have both committed a great sin, I feel as if the pleasure had not been too dearly bought, but for fear of discovery, hurry back to your own room.' And kissing me affectionately, both on mouth and prick, she prevailed upon me to take my leave of her for the time.

I had no sooner got outside the room and pulled the door to after me than I was struck dumb with surprise and fear, for I found my own chamber door open, and I felt certain that I had not been such a ninny as to leave it so. I entered the room on tiptoe, in fear and trembling, and found De Vaux standing by the window, looking white and thoughtful.

'Hello,' I said, 'what, in the devil's name, brings you here?'

'I came back,' he replied, 'to fetch some large shot which I had in my other shooting pouch.'

'Well, you've lost your bet,' I said triumphantly.

'I know it,' he gloomily made answer, 'and what worries me is I cannot understand it. You are not a better looking man than I am. Except in the matter of a few thousands a year and a larger tool, nature, luck and birth have not favoured you more than me, yet you absolutely mount a woman you have only known forty-eight hours, while I have for three long years tried in the same direction, and utterly failed. I will let you have the pin tomorrow.'

'But you only saw me coming from her room, how do you know that I absolutely won the trick?'

'How do I know? Why, I opened your door quietly to see if you were asleep, and finding you absent I looked around, and saw Mrs. Leveson's door open. I also heard you both hard at it, and could not forbear from peeping in. Oh, what a sight it was; there was she, lovely thing that she is, rising to every stroke, and I could see your long prick actually coming clear out of her, reculer pour mieux sauter, and then dashing in again till the sight nearly made a lunatic of me. How in the name of God did you work it, for it seems to me little short of miraculous?'

I didn't satisfy his curiosity, but left him to ponder over it, while I wrapped myself up, for the morning was getting chilly, and fell asleep.

De Vaux proceeded to the battue, but if his shooting was not superior to his spirits, the birds must have had a distinctly fine time of it, for if ever there was a man at a country luncheon table possessed by the megrims, De Vaux was that individual when I met him a few hours later.

CHAPTER 17

DE VAUX'S CHAGRIN A PROSTITUTION

During the afternoon, as good luck would have it, a wire from Hull (Oatlands Hall was thirty miles from that town) came to Mr. Leveson, desiring him to repair there to meet an old college chum who was passing through the sea port en route for Norway. So about five o'clock we had an early dinner, and wished him goodbye until the following day.

Mrs. Leveson had a splendid voice, and as two other musical friends dropped in later on, we had a most harmonious evening.

Towards ten o'clock, while I was turning over Mrs. Leveson's music for her, I seized an opportunity to whisper'Shall I come in to you, or will you visit a poor bachelor tonight?'

'The latter,' she replied, and blushed up to the roots of her hair. She had not yet learned how to deaden the qualms of conscience, but she was woman enough to intimate, very sotto voce,' We should be observed if we whispered any more.' Then, aloud, 'Mr. De Vaux, would you mind turning over for me, Mr. Clinton is so very awkward.'

This was the cut direct, before three others, too, but I grinned and bore it.

'She did not find you so awkward this morning, Clinton,' he whispered, as he leisurely took his stand by the piano, and I passed into the adjoining apartment where lay a 'cut-and-come-again* supper, to which I did ample justice.

About eleven o'clock, the guests having gone, Mrs. Leveson bade us both good-night in a stately, formal way and retired, and De Vaux and I proceeded to the billiard-room.

'I have a proposition to make you,' he said as he was chalking his cue for a game.

I couldn't think what De Vaux's rather serious manner imported, but at first imagined he was sore at losing his pin, and as my intrigue had been so delicious, I told him I knew what he was about to say, and that he might keep the heirloom (for I always believed it was an heirloom); I didn't really want it, and pointed out that he could salve his conscience in not paying the bet, as I had won it under circumstances which savoured of unfairness, but De Vaux stopped me.

'Let us sit down,' he said. 'I hardly feel in the humour for the green cloth tonight. Listen to me a few minutes.'

I sat down, curious to know what was coming next.

'The pin is yours, Clinton,' he said, 'and I have even forgotten that I ever possessed such a thing, but I wish to speak to you upon another matter.'

'My dear De Vaux,' I said, 'wait until I have lighted another cigar. Now, fire, away.'

'You are, as you justly call yourself, a Cunt Philosopher; lately I have gone in for arse castigation a good deal, and the passion that I once had for the more genuine article I foolishly imagined had died out.'

'What the devil does all this prelude mean, old man?'

'Simply this. Three years ago I was seriously, nay madly, in love with Mrs. Leveson. I would have given my finger tips to possess her, and when I made advances which were spurned, and eventually proceeded to extremes which resulted in my being politely told to make myself scarce, I was cut up more than I have been in my life, either before or since.'

'What damned nonsense you are talking, De Vaux.'

'I'm speaking the sober truth, Clinton. I accepted Leveson's invite down here thinking I had got over my foolish passion, but before I had been in her company ten minutes I had all the old feeling come back again with renewed force, and knowing how hopeless was the endeavour to become possessor of her charms, I made up my mind to cut short my visit.'

'What noble, lofty sentiment is this, my worthy friend; I'll be shot if I can understand it.'

'When I came in and discovered you this morning, the first feeling that predominated was rampant jealousy, and I really believe that, had I not governed myself by walking hastily away from the scene, I should have shot both of you.'

'Damn it, man, the bet was of your own making.'

'I know it, and I cursed myself as a blasted idiot for having made it, and then calmer thoughts prevailed. Now, as you have enjoyed one of the divinest women that was ever cast in beauty's mould, I want you to do me a good turn. I have, I think, without wishing to remind you of obligations rendered, done you one or two services in the fucking line.'

I remembered Lucy, and at once acquiesced.

'Tonight, knowing what I did, I watched you and Mrs. Leveson, and although I heard no words spoken, am quite sure that at the piano you arranged an assignation.'

'I did.'

'In your bedroom, or hers?'

'In my own.'

'Clinton, be a good friend,' De Vaux said earnestly, 'let me take your place.'

'She will find you out,' I said, not altogether falling in with his view, for although I had guessed what he was leading up to, I didn't quite relish the situation.

'What if she does, it will not matter once I am well in her; she won't cry out, that I can bargain for.'

'Well,' I said, 'how do you propose to work it?'

'Simply in this way: I take your bed, you take mine.'

'Right you are,' I said, and I really meant to oblige poor De Vaux at the time, but I was always a practical joker, and as I knew Hannah, the dread of her master having been removed, would be sure to run up within an hour of my retiring, I looked forward to some fun.

CHAPTER 18

RINGING THE CHANGES

We wished each other good-night, exchanging rooms as agreed, and acting upon my advice, De Vaux extinguished his candle, for fear of Mrs. Leveson coming in too soon. I waited to hear him piddle and get into bed, and then undressing myself, hastily crossed over to my darling.

She was lying propped up by the pillows, reading Ovid's Art of Love, a book I had seen in the library, and during the evening had recommended to her.

'Dear Mr. Clinton, I thought I was to come to you.'

'No, my precious,' I said, 'the bed is too narrow, and De Vaux sleeps so lightly he might hear us.'

As I said this I lifted the bedclothes lightly off her, and found that with natural bashfulness she had gone to bed in her drawers.

'Off with those appendages, my love,' I said.

'Oh, Mr. Clinton, don't be indecent; my modesty forbids.'

'Julia,' for I had ascertained her name, 'take off those stupid hindrances to love's free play, or wait, let me take them off for you.' And you would have laughed to have seen me executing this feat, for I lingered so long around her cunt every time I approached it, that it took me a good five minutes.

All this time Julia was fairly on fire, for the sight of my huge prick, as upright as a recruiting sergeant, would have excited Minerva herself.

'Now, my darling,' I said, 'let us have a little eccentricity. I understand both you and your husband want a youngster; now just tell me, does he ever have connection with you except in the old-fashioned way-belly to belly?'

'Never Mr. Clinton. How can there be any other method?'

'Good God,' I said, 'what venal innocence. Look here, my pet, kneel down as if you were praying for a family.' She did so.

'Now, clutch the iron rail at the foot of the bed, and put the top of your head hard down on this pillow, as if you were going to try to stand on it.'

'My dear Mr. Clinton, why all these preliminaries? I'm dying for it.'

'You shan't have long to wait, my pretty one.' For as she had minutely obeyed my instructions, her fair, round arse towered high in the bed, and I could just see the little seam of her vagina peeping at me from underneath.

Drawing back my foreskin until my best friend's top nut stood out like a glistening globe, quivering with excitement, I cautiously approached her, for I would have it understood, gentle reader, that tyros in cohabitation should always be cool when engaged in this particular style of sport.

'Straddle your knees slightly, my sweet one,' I whispered.

'For God's sake hasten, Mr. Clinton, this delay is killing me.'

Drawing back once more to allow the candlelight to play on the spot, so that I could not miss my mark, I thrust forward, and got the tip well placed for the final rush, but Julia anticipated me by suddenly squatting backwards, and for the moment I thought my bollocks and all had gone in.

Then commenced one of the most memorable fucks in my life's long record, and certainly one of the most pleasurable.

Every time I felt the inclination to spend I purposely stayed myself on the threshold of bliss in order to prolong.

At last, after Julia had saturated me three times, and was beginning to get pumped out, I brought all my forces to the charge, and giving several decisive lunges, which meant mischief, I fairly bathed her womb in boiling sperm, and the way that solid queen-like cunt closed on my prick, and held it as though we twain were one flesh, convinced me that the estate of Oatlands would in less than a year been fete, and the joy bells of the old village steeple would ring out to tell of a birth at the Manor House.

In the meantime, what had been going on in my own bedroom?

It had fallen out precisely as I had predicted.

Hannah had sneaked upstairs, and had slid into my bed, and De Vaux, without speaking, had fucked her with the dash and genuine passion born of a three years' forlorn hope.

Nor did he discover his mistake even after it was all over, for having in his ecstasy shagged her twice in ten minutes, he allowed her to escape, merely whispering in her ear that he hoped she had enjoyed it.

Hannah, on the contrary, had found out the imposture the moment she got De Vaux's prick in her. She had never felt but two, the coachman's and mine, and De Vaux's, although long and sinewy, was no match for either of ours in point of build; still it was better than not being fucked at all, and as De Vaux's ardent imagination was riding Mrs. Leveson, the servant got all the benefit, and not only prudently preserved her incognito, but lifted her brawny arse in such rare style that De Vaux was more than satisfied.

In the morning I went in to see him before proceeding downstairs; he shook hands with me cordially.

'Did she disappoint you?' I asked, with feigned innocence.

'My dear Clinton, she's a perfect angel, and you're a trump.'

Leveson came back the next day, and I never got another chance of landing Mrs. Leveson, who had fallen enceinte by me, and presented her husband with a son and heir nine months to the day.

De Vaux fondly imagines the kid must be his, and I am quite willing that he should continue to think so, but every time Leveson compares dates he thinks of his night's stay at Hull, shakes his head, and mutters that 'it's damned extraordinary', yet he wouldn't consider it at all extraordinary if he knew as much as we do, reader. What do you think?

CHAPTER 19

CONCERNING SIXTY-NINE OR THE MAGIC INFLUENCE OF THE TONGUE

The 'gamahuching' process should only be employed as a preliminary and never should be permitted to go to the extent of more than starting the tap. No woman living is able to withstand a moist and well-trained tongue. Even those in whom desire has long been dead have been known to shriek for the relief only an erect penis can afford.

Jack Wilton, the greatest essayist on cunt in an analytical form who ever lived, goes further, and even says-'a judicious tongue can galvanise into life a female corpse'.

This, of course, I do not admit, but there is a well-authenticated instance of a Somersetshire farmer's wife, who had fallen into a trance and was believed by all her neighbours to be dead, being recalled to life simply through the husband giving her fanny one last loving lick.

It is astonishing how prevalent the habit of gamahuching has become in England, and I would, while touching on it, maintain that there is nothing unnatural in it.

A tongue, soft and fleshy, fits in the vagina as though made for it, and though it can only titillate the clitoris, it serves the useful office of a vant-courier to the prick. The proof, if proof were wanting, that there is a distinct physical sympathy between the latter and the tongue, is that in the case of syphilis the tongue is affected almost as soon as the penis shows signs of having made a mistake. The proof again of its being natural to animal life is the fact that if one carefully observes the collection in the zoo it will be seen that when the beasts are in dalliance with one another the male invariably licks over the vagina of the female before proceeding to business.

This is my own observation, but if my readers doubt the statement, a run up to Regent's Park and a few hours in front of the cages will generally corroborate it.

I think to watch a man 'gamahuching' a woman is more

exciting than to see her being absolutely poked.

I remember staying on one occasion at a hotel in Paddington where a very pretty chambermaid showed me my room. I had not extinguished my candle more than five minutes before I heard a woman's voice in the next room 'Are you going to sit up reading all night?'

I couldn't for the life of me understand this, and thought the wall must be very thin, but it arose from the fact that some distance up the oaken partition there was a hole, caused through a good sized knot in the wood falling out, and although this hole had a coat hanging in front of it, I very speedily discovered it. It did not take me very long to remove the coat, and I saw the welcome light gleam through. Then, standing on a chair, I applied my eye to the hole, and saw a man leisurely undressing, and a ladylike woman, about thirty, with a splendid head of hair, lying quietly in bed awaiting him.

Now, I thought, there is going to be some fun, when a slight knock at my own door caused me to get down and open it.

'A telegram came for you two hours ago, sir, and they forgot to give it to you at the desk.'

'One moment, my girl,' I said, hastily slipping on my trousers and lighting my candle. The chambermaid was on the point of bolting. 'Don't go, my girl,' I said, 'there may be an answer to this; wait until I read it, and listen'-then, lowering my voice to a significant whisper – 'if you want to see a sight that will interest and amuse you, get on that chair and peep through the hole.'

'I daren't, sir, I should lose my situation if anyone were to know I was in a gentleman's bedroom.'

'I'll swear I won't harm you,' I said, and I really didn't intend to, for although the girl was a perfect little beauty, only sixteen and a half, I had done a long railway journey that day, and felt knocked up.

The girl hesitated for a moment, but as sincerity was prominent in the tones of my voice, and she was burning with curiosity to see what was going on, she quietly stepped into the room, and I helped her on to the chair.

'Stay,' I whispered. 'The candle must be extinguished, or

they may see you, if they have put theirs out.'

So saying I placed the room in darkness, and there was the light streaming through the hole. Mary, for such the soubrette called herself, immediately peeped.

For at least ten seconds she never stirred, then, getting another chair, I placed it by the side of Mary's and stood on it, with one arm around her waist.

What was going on in the next room I could only guess by the palpitation of Mary's heart. At last I said, 'May I peep, my dear?'

'Oh sir, wait a moment, I never saw such a thing in my life, do wait a moment.'

'Certainly, my angel, if you wish it,' I said; then taking her hand, which was trembling all over, I gently allowed it to rest on my prick, over which by this time I had lost complete control.

She clutched it wildly, and passed her hand all around the balls, then pulled the skin back, and so proved to me in less than three seconds that her exclamation just now might be a little bit qualified.

'Oh sir,' she said at length as I passed my hands up her petticoats and found her quim quite damp with excitement, 'I shall be missed downstairs. I must be going, but I should like to see the end of this.'

'You shall feel the end of this,' I said, 'and that's much more to the purpose.'

So, helping her down, I lifted her neatly on my bed, and planted it with such force that she cried out with the pain. But, whenever I have a new thing in cunts, I am always perfectly reckless of consequences, and so I gave no heed to her ejaculations, but fucked her to the bitter end.

Personally, I enjoyed it thoroughly, but I question very much whether she did, as the next morning she came to see me in a most disconsolate manner, and said she was afraid she would have to go to the hospital as I had completely split her cunt; but a 'tenner' soon squared that, and I would remark here that I have introduced this incident merely to show that the sight of a woman being 'gamahuched' is for more exciting than witnessing an ordinary fuck.

Had it been the latter that Mary had glanced at when she mounted the chair, she might have felt a passing interest, but it would have been no novelty. She would probably have called me a dirty beast, fled the apartment, and had a jolly good laugh over the adventure with the cook, but being a new sensation she was glued to the aperture, got excited, and had the implement put in her hand to quiet her.

It is true that she was a bad judge of size, or she might have hung back, but a split-up cunt is no great misfortune, since once the soreness has passed away it enables a woman to enter upon any amorous encounter without the fear of meeting a foe too big for a fair fight.

CHAPTER 20

AN ADVENTURE AT FOLKESTONE; THE YOUNG WIFE AND HER STEPDAUGHTER

Generally I have not been considered a very plucky man, but an event that occurred about this time almost caused me to believe in my own courageous qualities. I have since, however, in reviewing the past, come to the conclusion that it was sheer devilry, and the mad obliviousness of consequences which supervenes when an excited prick will not listen to the calmer instincts of reason.

I had run down to Folkestone for a brief holiday, and was staying at a large house on the Lees. I had taken the drawing-room floor, which consisted of the drawing-room itself, facing the sea, a large bedroom and a smaller one, which I used as a dressing-room.

An old general, who had recently come from India, and who in days gone by had been accustomed to put up with Mrs. Jordan, the landlady, applied for apartments, but as there were only two rooms to let, and he had a young wife and a growing daughter, it was quite impossible to accommodate him. I learned this accidentally through the landlady's daughter, with whom I was cultivating an intimacy that I hoped would develop into something sultry eventually, and immediately offered to give up my bedroom and sleep in the dressing-room.

The general was apprised of this, and was naturally charmed with my good nature.

A friendship was struck up over a weed, and the old nabob, in the course of a few days, settled down with his family, to whom he introduced me.

I did not know which to admire most. The wife, Mrs. Martinet, was a petite blonde, with those lovely violet eyes which change to a grey in the sunlight, just the sort of large reflective orbs historians ascribe to that darling Scottish queen who was fonder of a fuck than any woman born since the days of Bathsheba.

The daughter, Miss Zoe Martinet, was tall and queen like, dark with the suns of Hindustan, but with a splendid cast of countenance, which seemed to indicate that her Aryan mother had been one of the high caste women of India, who had lapsed with the gay English general when he was plain Colonel Martinet, twenty years before, and while the Grand Gordon and the Star of India were unknown to his breast.

The general was a confiding old fellow, but at sixty-eight one should not trust a wife of twenty-three with a stranger, especially when the stranger boasts a prick which, fully extended and in form, will touch the tape at eight inches.

Every day we went for long walks. General Martinet was very fond of going over to the officers' quarters at Shomcliffe, but although Eva and I were frequently left alone, her society and conversation were so intellectual and refined that I was in a dilemma how to open the ball.

One day, however, as she sat on the beach sewing, the opportunity occurred.

'What a lovely child,' she said, as a little girl of some three summers toddled by with a handful of flowers for some waiting mamma.

'Yes, lovely, indeed,' I said. 'Someday or another I hope to have the pleasure of seeing one with your face and eyes, and if it should be a boy I should take a delight in him for the sake of his mother. You are very fond of children, are you not?'

'Passionately,' she murmured.

'I thought so,' I observed. 'I have often remarked the absorbing interest you appear to take in babies with their nurses on the beach. How long have you been married?'

'Three years'-this with a sigh.

'Three years, good gracious! What time you have been wasting.'

She looked down at her embroidery, and became very interested in a wrong stitch.

'It is too bad of the general,' I continued, 'much too bad. I don't think I should have allowed you to wait all this time.'

'Mr. Clinton, what do you mean?'

'Do not feel angry, Eva, if you will forgive my calling you

that dear name; what I mean is this: that you are a woman fond of children and, therefore, formed to be a mother, and in not obeying the voice of nature and becoming one, you are offending against the divine law which teaches one to procreate.'

'I have tried, Mr. Clinton'-this in a whisper, with a deep blush- 'and have failed.'

'Say, rather,' I said, now thoroughly excited, 'the general has, and it is not your fault; but, my dear girl, every man is not verging on three score and ten, and we have not all, thank God, been desiccated on the scorching plains of Hindustan.'

'Mr. Clinton, do not tempt me!'

'Eva, it is your duty. If the old general were to have a son, your future would be secured. On the other hand what security have you that at the end of a few years he may not die, leaving all his fortune to his half-breed, ladylike daughter, Zoe?'

'That is very true,' she said, 'but still I don't think I could deceive him.'

Our conversation was prolonged for another half-hour, and when I retired to rest that night I had lovely visions, in which the landlady's daughter, Zoe and Eva were all mixed up higgledy-piggledy, but I had an indistinct idea when I awoke that I had not been idle during the night, for I seemed to remember performing on two of them, and it was only the cold sea-water bath that brought me to my senses, and made me lose that great lump of muscle at the bottom of my belly, till I began to believe that I should have had to pick it out with a pin-periwinkle fashion.

CHAPTER 21

WHERE IGNORANCE IS BLISS OR HAPPINESS IN AN ARMCHAIR

The general was a great gourmand, fond of sitting over his dinner a long time. The following day, after the conversation related in the last chapter, he invited me to share the repast with him, and after the meal regaled me with long stories of his conflict with the Sepoys and other natives of India.

'Why, sir,' he said to me, pointing to a pair of revolvers on the mantelpiece, 'Zoe's mother once fell into the hands of three vagabonds, and I shot them all and rescued her with those very weapons. That was how we became acquainted, and I would do as much today, old as I am, to any blackguard who dared insult her daughter.'

I cordially agreed with him that such would be only a just retribution, but I inwardly added that Zoe's cunt would be worth running the risk for.

After this we rejoined the ladies in the drawing-room as I had insisted on their using that apartment. After sitting there and chatting for about half an hour the general dozed off into a heavy sleep, and Zoe asked her stepmother to come out for a little while.

This Mrs. Martinet declined to do, on the ground that it was slightly chilly, so Zoe, who was a wilful specimen of womanhood, wished us au revoir and sallied forth.

I then poured out a glass of port, for Eva rather liked that wine, and unobserved by her, dropped out of my waistcoat phial enough Pinero Balsam to have stimulated an anchorite.

'Do have half a glass, I entreat you; it will put life in you. I have remarked that you seemed languid today.'

'Well, I will just take a wee drop,' said Eva, and she half emptied the glass as she spoke.

'Your husband sleeps soundly, Eva.'

'Hush; don't call me that here. Yes, he always sleeps so after dinner for a good half-hour.'

I was sitting in the armchair during this colloquy; Eva was

standing by the window, and I could just reach her skirt by leaning forward. I did so, and with both hands gently, but with adroit force, pulled her backwards, until she sat upon my lap.

'For God's sake,' she whispered in an agony of dread, 'let me go; if he were to wake he would kill us both.'

'But he won't awake. You told me yourself he would be sure to sleep for half an hour, and there is ample time for what we want to do in that space. Come into my bedroom for five minutes, my darling.'

'Mr. Clinton, I dare not; think of the exposure.'

'I can think of nothing but this, my sweet Eva,' and suiting the action to the word, I clapped my hand upon her lovely rosebud of a snatchbox before she had the slightest idea that I was anywhere near it.

She proved a game girl; she didn't cry out, for that would have meant death and damnation, but she appealed to my good sense.

'Not now,' she said imploringly, 'be counselled by me; not now, some other time.'

'My darling,' I said, 'stand up for one moment.' She did so, and I instantly lifted all her clothes, having in the meantime brought out my stiff straight cock, which I was mortally afraid would discharge its contents before it was properly positioned.

'Now sit down, dear.'

She obeyed me, and as she did so, I opened with the thumb and finger of my left hand the delicate sprouting lips; her arse did the rest, and I went in with a rush that made my very marrow twitter with pleasure.

'Oh God,' burst from Eva's lips, 'this is heavenly.'

The old man turned uneasily on the couch; the back of the armchair was turned to him, so that all he could see was the top of Eva's head.

'Is that you, Eva?' said the General.

'Yes, dear,' replied his wife.

'What are you doing, my love?'

'Still embroidering your new smoking cap, dear.'

'Where's Clinton?'

'He's gone out for a smoke,' said the trembling girl.

'All right, call me in half an hour.' And in less than three minutes the dear old soldier was once more in the Land of Nod, but during the three minutes we seemed to have lived an age. I would have gladly got out of her and sneaked away, for I could not help thinking of the revolvers, but she had never tasted the exquisite bliss a young man's prick can convey, and was, to use a 'servant galism', rampageous for it. She had never had a fuck before in such a position, but women are quick to learn a lesson when sperm is to be the prize, and in less than a minute she had wriggled out of me more genital juice than had ever rushed up my seminal ducts before. When she found she could draw no more, she quietly rose and walked to the window, leaving me to button up and vanish on tiptoe out of the drawing-room.

CHAPTER 22

THE MYSTERIOUS NOTE AND FRENCH LETTER SEQUEL

The reader knows my character by this time sufficiently well to be fully aware that I did not permit a single opportunity to escape of performing on Eva, till I think that young lady grew to look for it as regularly as a cat watches for the advent of a horseflesh purveyor.

One morning, however, I did not keep my appointment with her as usual, for we generally went out about midday, as I had found a quiet cowshed in a field on the Dover Road, behind which the grass grew thick and long, and there we were free from interruption.

There, too, if there be any truth in the general belief that semen is a great fructifier of the soil, the grass should grow thicker than ever by this time, for I am sure that Eva and I had bathed it with the best essence we possessed.

This particular morning, however, I received a note in a handwriting I did not know; the letter ran thus:

SIR
Your liaison with Mrs. M- is known, and it depends upon you whether it will be divulged to her husband. Meet me near the spot you generally meet her, at two p.m. today.
Yours,
ONE WHO HAS SEEN ALL

It was a woman's hand, and I was puzzled. I dropped a few lines to Eva, saying I could not keep my appointment with her and proceeded to the rendezvous to find my fair anonyma.

I arrived at the back of the cowshed and turned the corner to find to my intense surprise Zoe standing there, in her hands a bunch of fresh wild flowers; as she was expecting me, whereas I had never dreamed that it was she who had sent the note, she had me at a decided disadvantage.

'Well, sir,' she said, 'you received my communication?'

'I did,' I replied, 'and I'm sorry to think you have seen all, for I was hoping someday to afford you the novelty of examining it.'

'Mr. Clinton, how could you have been so wicked? My poor old father is not far from the grave; you might have waited until Eva had been left a widow.'

If you look at me another moment with those flashing eyes I shall do you over in the same way, my pet, I thought.

'Let us sit down and reason, Miss Martinet; you have chosen a strange place for a serious conversation, but it will be infinitely better for you to sit down and then the tall grass will conceal you from view, whereas standing up every country yokel who passes by sees us both, puts his own construction on it, and your reputation is irretrievably ruined.'

'You are perfectly right,' said Zoe. 'I will sit down, especially as I note some uniforms on the road yonder, and they might be officer friends of my father's.'

Zoe sat down and put up her parasol, but the two gentlemen she had remarked came around the head of me road at the same time. They were two lieutenants of the – th, at Dover, and I had been at a ball where I had knocked up against them some little time before.

'Hello! Clinton, what the devil are you-Oh, I say-a petticoat. Well, I'm damned-alfresco, eh? under the azure dome of heaven. Well, good luck, my boy; but give me a pair of nice clean sheets and native nakedness.' And down the road went the pair, humming a godless tune they had picked up in the camp before Sebastopol a few years before.

I turned to Zoe.

'What a fortunate thing you were out of sight, my dear,' I said, sitting down beside her.

'Yes, it was, indeed,' she said, trying with her short skirt to conceal a shapely ankle, which, in a pair of elegant scarlet stockings, looked simply delicious.

I know it was very rude and ungentlemanly of me, but I could not help remarking aloud what an exquisite tournure the stocking gave to her leg, and enquired whether she thought the colour had anything to do with it.

'Mr. Clinton, I think we had better go,' was all the answer she gave me.

'But, my dear Zoe, I thought you had brought me here to read me a prim lecture on morality?'

'Alas!' she said, sighing, 'I could not tell on poor dear mamma, she is so artless, and-'

'And I am so artful, you would say; but, my dear young lady, I admit to having made a great mistake in intriguing with the general's wife, I can see it now.'

'And I hope,' she said, making a pretty bow, 'that you are contrite?'

'Yes,' I said, 'I am, but shall I explain to you the error I committed?'

'If it will not take too long in the telling.'

'Well, my mistake was in going for the wife, and not the daughter.'

'Mr. Clinton, how can you say such a thing?'

'Zoe, from the moment I first saw your matchless face, your eyes burned into my bosom's core like fire, and now, by heaven, that we are here alone, with none but bright Phoebus as our witness, I must-' Here commenced a struggle in the grass, but it was of short duration.

She threatened to scream, but I hurriedly pointed out that if she accused me of rape I could bring the two young officers as witnesses that I had a lady with me who was sitting on the grass apparently only waiting for it, and besides-but all my entreaties were of no avail. At length, growing desperate, and with a prick on me like a bull's pizzle, I forced her legs apart, and would have ravished her by sheer strength, had she not whispered in my ear – 'For God's sake use a French letter; I'm so afraid of falling in the family way.'

Now I never slip from home without a letter, but I hate using them when I know the cunt is fresh and untainted with any soupcon of forethought. The fact that the request came from one I had supposed a virgin rather astounded me, but I was fully equal to the occasion. Taking one from my waistcoat pocket, and beginning to fit it on, I said, 'Then you've had the root before,

Zoe.'

'Yes,' she said, 'once, with a young captain in my pa's regiment at Allahabad, but this was when I was seventeen. He always used them for fear of the consequences.'

By this time I had fitted it, and Zoe showed her perfect readiness to wait patiently for the operation.

'Let me have one peep, darling,' I said.

She laughingly lay back flat on her back, and showed me a large forest of hair, as glossy as a raven's back and as black, while beneath it I saw as neat a little quimbo as one could wish for.

Reader, do you blame me if, after seeing such a sight, I surreptitiously pulled off the letter and let my John Thomas approach his lairau nature. I should have been more than mortal to have refrained. Flesh is a hundred per cent better than a nasty gutta-percha cover, and although Zoe was unaware of what I had done, she showed herself fully appreciative of my premier thrust, though her action took me completely by surprise.

Whether it was the springiness of the soft green grass on which we lay, I know not, but with all my experience I cannot recall to mind any wench, even one having her first grind, who showed such arse-power as Zoe.

The Hindu and English cross must be a good fucking breed, I thought, but scarcely had the fleeting idea passed through my brain than one more vigorous push brought on the crisis of delight.

Zoe, at this point, was working her bottom with what the Yankees would call an 'all-hellfire motion', when she suddenly seemed transported with delight, and kissing my neck, bit me in a frenzy till she actually brought forth blood.

Much as I had enjoyed myself, this was a style of emotion I was not enamoured of, and I screamed out with the pain.

I had got up, leaving Zoe still lying exhausted on the ground, when to my horror I heard a step behind me, and before I could button up found myself confronted by Eva.

I do not know why it should have been so, but although the meteorological record for that year does not return the weather in May as being particularly warm, I found it at least 212° Fahrenheit on that eventful day, in spite of the sea breeze-so not liking tropical heat, I returned to town. I have met Zoe in society since, but poor Eva, after tasting forbidden fruit, and finding it so much sweeter than the withered-up stuff obtainable from her husband's orchard, went wrong again and again, and was finally bowled in the very act-but, luckily for the gay Lothario, the general had left those chased revolvers at home.

CHAPTER 23

A DISAGREEABLE MISTAKE

Not always have I had the happiness of being fortunate in my amours. It is true that I have managed to escape the dread fate of those poor unfortunate devils whose tools are living witness to the powers of caustic and the lethal weapons of surgery, but I have on occasions been singularly unfortunate, and as the warning voice of my publisher tells me I have little more time or space at my disposal, I will devote the present chapter of this work to detailing a most unpleasant incident of the sort which all people are more or less liable to who go in for promiscuous intercourse to any large extent.

My only sister, Sophy, came up to London with her husband shortly after my return from Folkestone, and although he was a perfect brute of a fellow, and a man I disliked very much, I made myself as agreeable as I could and took a furnished house for them during their stay, near the Regent's Park.

Frank Vaughan, a young architect and a rising man, was one I introduced them to, as my sister had brought a friend, Miss Polly White, with her, who lived near our old home in the country; being anxious for her to see London, her parents had placed her under my sister's guardian wing to do the 'lions' of the metropolis.

Polly was an only daughter, so knowing the old people had a good nest-egg, I thought it would be a capital opportunity to throw Frank in her way.

I told him precisely how matters stood, and advised him to make a match of it.

'The old people are rich,' I said, 'but if they object to you on the score of money, fuck her, my boy, and that will bring them to reason.'

'Is she perfectly pure now?' said Frank. 'For to tell you the truth I haven't come across a genuine maid since I landed a stripling of sixteen, nearly ten years ago. Are you sure you haven't?'

'I'll swear it, if you like,' I returned, laughing at the soft impeachment, 'but take my advice, Frank, and win her. She'll be worth at least forty thousand when the old folks snuff it.'

'I'm on the job,' said Frank; and it was easy to see from the immaculate shirt front, the brilliant conversation, and the great attention he paid her, that he meant business.

One night, however, I was puzzled, for I thought Frank was far more assiduous in his manner to my sister than he should have been, considering that the 'nugget', for so we had christened Polly, was present.

I could not understand it at all, and determined to watch the development of the situation.

There was, I must tell you, an underplot to all this, for several times I had noted that Polly's regard for me was a trifle too warm, and once or twice in the theatre, and in the brougham, coming home particularly, I had felt the soft pressure of her knees, and returned it with interest-but, to my story:

Frank proposed going to Madame Tussaud's, and as Polly had never been, and my sister knew every model in the show by heart, Frank suggested that he should take the 'nugget', 'unless you would like to go with us,' he said to me.

'Not I, indeed,' was my reply. 'Besides, Sissy here will be alone, as her beautiful husband has been out all day, and will, I suppose, return beastly drunk about midnight. No, you go together and enjoy your little selves.' So off they went.

When Polly passed me in the hall, she gave me a peculiar look, which I utterly failed to comprehend, and asked me to fasten her glove. As I did so she passed a slip of paper into my hand and when she had gone I read on it these words: 'Be in the study about nine o'clock.'

What can the little minx mean? was my first thought. She surely wouldn't go about an intrigue in this bare-faced fashion; she has been brought up in a demure way. Yet what on earth can she mean? At any rate I will do her bidding.

Making an excuse to my sister about eight o'clock, for I was as curious as possible to know what it could all portend, and saying I was going out for a couple of hours, I slammed the hall door behind me, and then quietly crept upstairs to the study.

I found it in darkness, but knowing where the couch was

situated, at the far end of the room, I made for it, and I must confess the solitude, the darkness and a good dinner, all combined, made me forget curiosity, Polly, the warning note and everything else, and in less than five minutes I was fast asleep.

I was awakened by a scented hand I knew was a woman's touching my face and a low voice whispered in my ear'You are here then; I never heard you come in.'

Damn it, I thought, it's an intrigue after all; but she's too tall for Polly. Oh, I see it all, she's our prim landlady (who retained one room in the house, and was, I knew, nuts upon my brother-in-law). Polly found out about it, and set me on the track, so without saying a word I laid her unresistingly on the couch, and in a few seconds was busy.

I could not help thinking while wiring in that she displayed much vigour for one of her years, since I judged the lady to be at least forty105 five, but her ardour only made me the more fervent, and at the end of a long series of skirmishes the real hot short work began.

It would be impossible to express my horror at this moment when my hand came in contact with a cross she was wearing around her neck, and I found that it was my own sister I was rogering.

I had, unluckily, got to that point where no man or woman could cease firing, but the worst part of the damned unfortunate affair was that I burst out with an ejaculation of dismay and she recognised my voice. The situation was terrible.

'Good God!' I said. 'Sophy, how on earth has this come about?'

Then, sobbingly, she told me that her husband had abstained from her for more than two years because he had contracted a chronic gonorrhoeic disorder and that Vaughan had won her over to make this rendezvous, and had intended letting Polly be shown through Tussaud's by a friend he had arranged to meet there. 'But,' she added, 'how was it I found you here?' This I dared not tell her, as it was now evident that Polly was aware of the assignation, and to let my sister know-that would have been death.

Poor girl, she was sufficiently punished for her frailty, and Polly, who had caught a few words of the appointment, was sufficiently revenged.

CHAPTER 24

REFLECTIONS ON 'AULD LANG SYNE', HAPPY MEETINGS, AND CONCLUSION

Fifteen years have now elapsed since I scribbled the former part of my experiences. Times are sadly altered with my best friend now, and I am rapidly approaching the time when all may prove 'vanity and vexation of spirit', for although I still carry a most formidable outward and visible sign, the inward and spiritual grace so necessary to please the ladies is now almost dormant in my fucked-out nature.

Years ago I remember how I looked with something like contempt upon the art and science of flagellation as dilated upon by Monsignor Peter; now I am quite converted to his theory.

A most fortunate recontre has been the means of this conversion; lately sauntering down Regent Street, thinking of the time when I used to do three or four pretty demi-mondes in a day'Ah, Gerty, do you know him, too?' in an ever to be remembered voice caused me suddenly to turn and confront the speaker, who proved to be none other than Airs Leveson, looking almost as lovely as ever, and incomprehensively in the company of my old flame Gerty, of the Temple. This was a delightful renewal of old acquaintanceships, and a very few explanations let me thoroughly into the situation.

Leveson had been dead several years, leaving his wife sole guardian of their son (my son, she assured me in a loving whisper. 'He is now eighteen-never can I forget the night you made him for me').

Gerty had been persuaded by Airs Leveson to give up her dressmaking business, and live with her as a kind of companion housekeeper, the former's Sapphic tastes having attached her to the voluptuous Airs L., who discovered it from Gerry's remarks on the women of the day in Paris, who prefer their own sex as lovers and care very little for the attentions of men.

'My son is abroad with his tutor; will you, Mr. Clinton, come home to dinner, and spend the evening at our quiet little town house? James is such a rake-just like his father-I don't mean Mr. Leveson, poor dear, he was rather too good, and never made a baby for me or anyone else. Gerty knows all about it, but your name was never mentioned, and now I suppose you are the Temple student who seduced her with finery, and took advantage of her young inexperience, although she never mentioned you?'

'Really, this is most charming, but, my dear ladies, I can only accept if you promise we shall be a happy family-free from jealousy.'

'Make yourself easy, dear Mr. Clinton; as to that, everything is common between us in thought, word and deed; in feet, with our dearest friend, Lady Twisser, we are three loving communists, each one's secrets as sacred as if our own!'

'Lady Fanny Twisser, who was separated from her husband because he couldn't believe his dildo was the father of her boy!' I exclaimed.

'Good God, Mr. Clinton, there you are again; you must be a universal father. Now I'm sure it's you who did that service for dear Fanny, and we'll wire to her at once to come and join our dinner party.'

Highly elated they conducted me to their carriage, which was waiting outside Lewis and Allenby's, and we soon reached Mrs. Leveson's house in Cromwell Road, South Kensington.

Gerty showed me to a room to prepare for dinner, and it was arranged we should have a real love seance after the servants had gone to bed. At dinner I saw Lady Fanny, who met me with a most fervent embrace, assuring me, with tears in her eyes, that I was the source of the only happiness she had had in her life (her son, now at Oxford).

All through dinner, and long after while we sat on over dessert talking of old times, I felt as proud as a barn-door cock with three favourite hens, all glowing with love and anxious for his attentions; the ardent glances of lovely Mrs. Leveson told too plainly the force of her luscious recollections, while Lady Fanny, who sat by my side, every now and then caressed my prick under the table, eliciting a slight throbbing in response to her touches.

At length coffee was brought in, and the servants told to go to bed.

'At last!' sighed our hostess, springing up and throwing her arms around my neck, 'I have a chance to kiss the father of my boy; what terrible restraint I have had to use before the servants. Dear James, you belong to us all, we all want the consolation of that grand practitioner of yours; have which of us you please first; there's no jealousy!'

'But, darling loves, how can I do you all? I'm not the man I was some years ago!'

'Trust in Gerry's science, for she let us into the Pinero Balsam secret, and we have a little of it in the house for occasions when it might be wanted. It's very curious how you ruined the morals of both Fanny and myself, two such paragons of virtue as it were; we could never forget the lessons of love you taught us, and, now we are both widows, with dear Gerty here, we do enjoy ourselves on the quiet. Fanny's boy has me, and thinks it is an awfully delicious and secret liaison; my James returns the kindness to my love's mother; while dear abandoned Gerty is only satisfied sometimes by having both with her at once, yet neither of them ever divulges their amour with Fanny and myself. And now, how is the dear jewel? You surely don't require the balsam to start with,' she said, taking out my staff of life, and kissing it rapturously. Lady Fanny did the same, and was followed by Gerty, whose ravishing manner of gamahuching me recalled so vividly my first seduction of her in the Temple. She would have racked me off, but I restrained myself, and requested them to peel to the buff, setting them the example, my cock never for a moment losing his fine erection.

Having placed an eider-down quilt and some pillows on the hearthrug, they ranged themselves in front of me in all their naked glories, like the goddesses before Paris disputing for the apple. 'Catch which you can,' they exclaimed, laughing, and began capering around me.

I dashed towards Airs Leveson, but tumbled over one of the pillows, getting my bottom most unmercifully slapped before I could recover myself. My blood tingled from head to foot. I was made to be into one of those luscious loving women, and in a moment or two caught and pulled down Fanny on top of me; the other two at once settled her, a la St George, and held my prick till she was fairly impaled on it. They then stretched themselves at full length on either side, kissing me ardently, while their busy fingers played with prick and balls, and the darling Fanny got quickly into her stride and rode me with the same fire and dash which characterised her first performance on her brother's bed in the Temple.

My hands were well employed frigging the creamy cunts of Mrs. Leveson and Gerty-what a fuck, how my prick swelled in his agony of delight, as I shot the hot boiling sperm right up to Fanny's heart, and she deluged me in return with the essence of her life as she fell forward with a scream of delight. Her tightly nipping cunt held me enraptured by its loving contractions, but at the suggestion of Gerty she gently rolled herself aside and allowed me to mount the darling Leveson before I lost my stiffness.

What a deep-drawn sigh of delight my fresh fuckstress gave, as she heaved up her buttocks and felt my charger rush up to the very extremes of her burning sheath.

'Let me have the very uttermost bit of it! Keep him up to his work, Gerty, darling,' she exclaimed excitedly, then gluing her lips to mine she seemed as if she would suck my very life away.

A smart, tingling, swish-swish on my rump now aroused me to the fact that both Fanny and Gerty had taken in hand the flagellation and, gradually putting more force in their cuts, they raised such a storm of lustful heat that I fucked dear Mrs. Leveson till we both lost consciousness for a time in an ecstatic agony of bliss and when we recovered ourselves declared that no such exquisite sensations had ever before so completely overwhelmed either of us.

Such was the power of the rod to invigorate me that Gerty soon had her cunt as well stuffed as the others had been by my grand prick, which seemed to be bigger and stiffer than ever.

This loving seance was kept up into the small hours of the morning before I could think of tearing myself from their seductive delights; but I now often join this community of love in the Cromwell Road and no pen can by any possibility adequately describe the delights we manage to enjoy under the influence of the birch.